D1391212

A PROPER LITTLE NOORYEFF

Jamie's blood ran cold ... tights? 'You'll find them much more comfortable. Nobody can dance in skin-tight jeans ... look at you! Can't even bend your legs properly.'

Jamie can't believe he has agreed to partner the ballet school's star pupil, Anita. He wasn't even interested in ballet – he was simply picking his sister up after her ballet lesson when he was persuaded to dance. Yet once he starts he finds he enjoys it. The only problem is ... what happens if his friends find out?

ABOUT THE AUTHOR

Jean Ure is one of the most distinguished authors writing for teenagers and children. She had her first novel published when she was fifteen and still at school, but spent two years at drama school and had a variety of jobs before turning to writing full-time. She has now written many highly-acclaimed novels.

Jean Ure lives in Surrey with her husband, two cats and three dogs.

A Proper Little
NOORYEFF

JEAN URE

HEINEMANN
NEW WINDMILLS

Heinemann Educational
a division of
Heinemann Publishers (Oxford) Ltd,
Halley Court, Jordan Hill, Oxford OX2 8EJ
OXFORD LONDON EDINBURGH
MADRID ATHENS BOLOGNA PARIS
MELBOURNE SYDNEY AUCKLAND SINGAPORE TOKYO
IBADAN NAIROBI HARARE GABARONE
PORTSMOUTH NH (USA)

The moral rights of the author
have been asserted.

© Jean Ure 1982

First published by The Bodley Head Ltd, 1982

First published in the New Windmill Series 1993

93 94 95 96 97 10 9 8 7 6 5 4 3 2

ISBN 0 435 12402 1

British Library Cataloguing in Publication Data
for this title is available from the British Library

Cover design Third Man
Cover illustration by Rod Holt

The play of A Proper Little Nooryeff by Jean Ure
is published by Cambridge University Press.

Printed and bound in England by Clays Ltd, St Ives plc

1

Cautiously, keeping one eye on Mr Hubbard, busy scrawling cabalistic symbols over the entire length of the blackboard, Jamie reached out for his pen. With the flat of his hand, he edged his geometry rough book towards him; between finger and thumb, turned the page. Old Mother Hubbard had ears like a lynx: if you only stopped breathing for five seconds he wanted to know what you were up to. Over on the far side of the room some great gormless prat was cracking his fingers. Crack, crack, flaming crack. They were going off like pistol shots. Any minute now and the Hubbard would be spinning round demanding to be told "Which of you louts is playing the percussion?"

He eased the top off his pen. It was the new felt tip he'd purloined from his little sister's pencil case that morning. A new felt tip always inspired confidence. Boldly, in big black capitals, he wrote WHAT ABOUT TOMORROW?, underlining each word very heavily three times, that there might be no mistake. Next to him, Doug Masters, who was supposed to be his best friend, craned over to see what he had written. He put his arm across it: this correspondence was private, even from best friends.

He waited till the next jet plane went thundering overhead, then with practised hand ripped out the page, at the same time as Doug stuffed his mouth full of biscuit and half a dozen whispered conversations were hurriedly resumed. Mr Hubbard, who hadn't been born yesterday, whipped round from the board.

The jet passed on, the roar died away. Mr Hubbard nodded, and went back to his symbols. Doug's jaws worked silently on undigested biscuit. Jamie folded his paper into a compact square and leaned across the gangway to prod at the nearest girl. (Old Mother Hubbard was a stickler for segregation. He said teenage boys were lower than beasts of the field, and that if he had his way they would all be kept in cages and regularly thrashed.)

The girl looked up, vacantly; disturbed, no doubt, from some private daydream. Jamie thrust the note at her. He pointed urgently at Sharon, sitting prim and upright in the front row, making as if the cabalistic symbols really turned her on. The girl shrugged her shoulders. Her name was Coral something. It always sounded like Coral Flashlight, but he supposed it couldn't really be. People just weren't called things like Flashlight. Anyway, it didn't matter what she was called, all he wanted was for her to get that note to Sharon.

Furtively, overdoing the cloak-and-dagger bit, she stretched an arm across the gangway, twisting her palm back to front like something out of a second-rate spy movie. The note, not surprisingly, fell to the ground. Jamie pushed at it with the toe of his shoe: maladroitly, she raked it in with her ruler, a feat ten times more difficult than simply leaning over to pick it up. Anxiously he watched its passage down through the ranks to the front row. He saw it placed on Sharon's desk. He saw her glance at it – cool, disparaging. What is this rubbish? He could imagine

2

the disdainful lift of the eyebrow. Sharon was good at disdainful lifts of the eyebrow. Jamie put a finger in his mouth and tore at a flap of loose skin. The note lay where it was, in full view of the Hubbard should he choose to turn round and cast his gaze in that direction. For one agonizing moment he thought the little cow wasn't even going to bother reading it – thought she might even be going to humiliate him in front of the whole goggling harem by simply screwing it up; but then, slowly, with an air of bored condescension, as if the whole business were too utterly childish for words, she slid it off the desk and down into her lap. He saw the dip of her head as she switched her eyes away from the board, and he knew that she was at least going to look at it. That, at any rate, was something.

Mr Hubbard, going a bit manic, started banging chalk against the board, viciously stabbing letters of the alphabet into the various nooks and crannies of his symbols, droning some geometric liturgy to himself as he did so. Some gobbledygook about hypotenuses. Jamie spared the thing one quick glance, then returned his attention to Sharon. She seemed to be writing a reply. He hadn't expected that. At worst he had expected her to ignore him; at best, if she happened to be in a good mood, he had thought she might perhaps turn round and nod; but he hadn't expected the favour of an actual reply. Sharon thought old Mother Hubbard was the cat's whiskers. That was why she always sat up straight and studied his symbols and tried to pretend she was some kind of mathematical genius. She wasn't given to messing about with notes, as if they were still in junior school.

By the same devious route as it had gone out, his sheet of paper made its way back to him. Sharon was already doing her little Goody Two Shoes bit again; not even bothering to turn round in her seat. Somehow, he felt that it did not bode well. Coral Flashlight, with her eyes fixed firmly to the front, leaned across the gangway and dropped the folded square upon his desk lid. Just in time, he pushed it under his rough book, as Mr Hubbard spun round and said: "Right! Pay attention! Given that angle A is 110° – "

Never mind angle A; there were more important things at stake. Like, what about tomorrow? If that little cow were going to let him down –

He wiped a lock of hair out of his eyes. Mr Hubbard turned back again, to embellish angle A. Doug, who had plainly been awaiting his opportunity, instantly nodded in Sharon's direction, and pulling a face like a demented gorilla began making a series of unmistakable gestures, right hand placed in the crook of his left elbow, left hand clenched into a fist. Broad grins ran like an attack of mumps about the classroom. Even some of the harem were giggling; others, as usual, were looking down their noses like rows of affronted dowagers. Some of the girls thought Doug was a riot. Some of them didn't.

Sharon herself remained oblivious, though had she seen she would not have been embarrassed. She would only have tossed her head in that way she had, full of female contempt for male stupidity. Jamie was the one who stood in danger of embarrassment. He could do without Doug's crudities, just at this moment. In any case, he'd got hold of the wrong end of the stick where Sharon was concerned. Straight up and down, that was Sharon. Strictly no funny business. It was hands off and a quick peck on the cheek if you were lucky. Not that he'd ever particularly wanted anything more. Really he only

4

kissed her because it was the thing to do; he'd have been quite happy without. Sometimes he thought that so would she.

Doug, encouraged by the mump-like grins, was growing pornographic. The big blue soup-plate eyes of Coral Flashlight protruded like globules: she tittered, into her hand. Jamie felt his cheeks turning brick colour. Savagely, he hacked at Doug's ankle beneath the desk. Doug only leered, and with maddening affability stuck his fingers in Jamie's face. There were times when having Doug for a best friend could be a real pain. Goaded, Jamie gave him a sharp shove in the ribs and mouthed two words, very succinctly. They were the sort of words which at home would have brought him a stiff clip round the ear and the advice to "Watch that language! You're not in a barrack room." Now they brought only the sarcastic invitation from the front of the class to "Feel quite free to express yourself, lad . . . no need to be bashful. If you've something to say, let's all have the benefit."

Coral Flashlight tittered again. Jamie squirmed.

"Well?" Mr Hubbard waited, expectantly. "*Do* you have something to say?" A pause. Doug wrote BALLS on the cover of his rough book. "You do not have something to say. Strange – I could have sworn I saw your lips move. Perchance you were but practising the art of silent ventriloquy? If that is the case, then I would strongly advise you for the future to stick to one of the lesser known foreign languages. Preferably Serbo-Croat. Not everyone is as robust as your friend Douglas. Now, I wonder, if it's not putting you to too much trouble, whether I might tempt you to direct your attention to the angle marked C in the far corner of the figure marked (i) upon the blackboard and advise us as to its probable

5

size? – You note I say probable. I am well aware that a wild guess is about to be unleashed upon us. Just strive, if you will, to apply at least a modicum of intelligence."

Sharon had half turned in her seat. He could feel her eyes upon him, round and brown and bright like a sparrow's. He wondered if they contained any faint glimmerings of sympathy, or only scorn.

"You have one in 180 chances," said Mr Hubbard. He said it bracingly. "That is a great deal better than the football pools."

"Football pools are a load of crap," said Doug.

One of the harem said: "That's all you know. My dad won fifty quid on them last year."

Someone else said: "My dad once got a postal order for a fiver and my mum went mad and stuck it on the mirror and couldn't get it off again."

Doug said: "It's a mug's game, doing the pools."

"Yes, and it's a mug's game not paying attention in my geometry lessons." Mr Hubbard picked up a piece of chalk and lobbed it across the room at Jamie. "Come on, dozy! Look alive."

Mechanically, he fielded the piece of chalk. A faint, derisive cheer went up. Someone shouted: "Owzatt?" Mr Hubbard thumped on his desk.

"Shut up! I'm waiting for the Professor over here to set his powerful intellect in motion . . . angle C, Professor! Enlighten us, if you please."

Jamie wondered if little Goody Two Shoes sitting so smug in the front row knew what size the flaming angle was supposed to be. He certainly didn't. Taking a stab at random, he said: "Forty-five degrees."

"*Wrong!*" Mr Hubbard intoned it triumphantly, booming his voice like a gong. From somewhere down the front of the class came the sound of sycophantic sniggering. He knew, then, that whatever she had written in that note he wasn't going to like it. Mr Hubbard, playing to his audience, waved a careless hand. "Oh, sit down, lad! Sit down! Take the pressure off your brain . . . you'll do yourself a mischief, standing there like that."

Jamie sat down. Under cover of the laughter which greeted this latest shining example of wit and repartee, he slid the sheet of paper from under his rough book. Surreptitiously, he prised open a corner of it. A corner was enough. Under the big bold capitals of his WHAT ABOUT TOMORROW? Sharon's small, tight hand came back at him, insolently: *What about it?*

He seethed. It was only what he had half been expecting, but still he seethed. He spent the rest of the period seething. He would like to have gone marching down the gangway, lifted her bodily out of her seat, and shaken her till the teeth rattled in her little pea-brained head. He'd thought something was up, the way she'd been avoiding him. She'd been on her high horse all week, refusing to talk. She got like that, sometimes. Moody; spiteful. He didn't know why he bothered with her. She wasn't anyone special. There were plenty of other girls just as pretty, *and* with nicer natures. A pity she couldn't contract something hideous and disfiguring, like a plague of boils or an attack of mumps. He'd like to see her with her face all swollen up. That would show her. That would take her down a peg or two. Primping little madam.

He was still seething when the bell rang for break. Sharon, who usually stayed behind to ingratiate herself with the Hubbard, was up and out of the door before Jamie had even got his books together. By the time he had fought his way through the harem and out into the corridor, she had disappeared. He ran her to earth five minutes later, seated on a bench in the sunshine, safely surrounded by a gaggling horde. He glared at her from a distance: she stared back at him, haughtily. Later on, during the dinner break, he hung around outside the door of the girls' cloakroom, which was strictly not allowed, and tried to collar her as she came out, but she had obviously been anticipating an attempt of some sort because she had taken the precaution of arming herself with a friend. This time, the friend stared at him haughtily as well. He ignored her, and jerked his head at Sharon.

"Coming up the road?"

"Can't," said Sharon. "Got things to do."

"Can't," said the friend. "Got things to do."

They went off together, arm in arm. He heard them giggling, as they turned the corner. Why did girls always have to be so unpleasant?

A day which rounded itself off with a double dose of physics couldn't really be expected to have very much going for it, not even if it did come right at the end of the week. Her Highness didn't take physics. If she had, he could at least have sat there and execrated her. As it was, he could only sit there and brood. Doug, slouched next to him on one of the lab's high stools, at the furthest end of the extremest back bench, which was their usual slouching place, drew obscenities in his phys. and chem. book and tried to interest him in a game of Filthy Limericks.

"There was a young woman from Bude – "

"Belt up."

"Who stood at a bus stop quite nude – "

"Look, I said belt up, didn't I?"

Doug stuck his fingers in his face.

"What's your problem?"

"Haven't got a problem."

"Old Miss Strait Lace given you the elbow?"

So what if she had? Jamie humped a shoulder and gazed moodily down the lab to where Miss Spender was doing things with a bell jar and a bit of limp balloon. What if she had? What did he care? He'd never really fancied her all that much. She was just someone to knock around with. You had to have someone, you couldn't tag along on your own; but truth to tell, he'd never been what you might call struck on her. She didn't exactly turn him on. Come to that, he couldn't think of any girl who did. He wasn't a raving sex maniac like Doug. He could take it or leave it. All the same, no one liked being stood up, and furthermore he didn't see why she was doing it to him. There wasn't anything wrong with him, was there? He didn't have bad breath, or body odour, or – for a ghastly moment he thought that he did, but it was only that great hulking idiot next to him, messing about with the Bunsen burner. Blow the place up, if he wasn't careful.

He looked at him, frowning. No girl, as far as he knew, had ever stood Doug up. What had Doug got that he hadn't? He wasn't any brainier, he wasn't an athlete, he hadn't got any hair on his chest. He had admittedly started shaving, but you had to look pretty hard to notice, and anyway, to counterbalance that he had pimples. Great red pimples that sometimes turned yellow. Jamie didn't have pimples. He didn't have a face like an old boot, either. A short while ago he'd actually overheard his Auntie Carol say to his mother that "Jamie's going to be quite nice-looking, isn't he?"

He scowled. The fact that she'd said *going* to be meant that she still regarded him as just a kid. Smooth, unformed. In that case he wasn't sure that he wanted to be "quite nice-looking". Sooner be mature and have a face like a boot. He bet if that little cow had been going out with Doug she wouldn't have dared treat *him* that way.

Doug caught his eye and winked.

"Cheer up . . . plenty more fish in the sea."

Well, *that* was an original remark.

On his way down to the cloakrooms at the end of the day he made a special detour via the Assembly Hall, where the house notice boards were to be found. He always did it, every Friday; never actually stopping to study them, in case people should see him and think "There he goes, poor mug, looking for his name again", but just casually strolling past and nonchalantly glancing as he did so. Today he glanced so nonchalantly that he had to go back and glance again, to make quite sure that he wasn't hallucinating.

He wasn't. It was up there, in black and white.

TEAM FOR INTERHOUSE MATCH WED. 12TH MAY
R. Pearson (Cap.)
D. Jones
J. Carr –

He'd made it! He'd flaming well *made* it! Out of the corner of his eye, he saw the swish of something yellow. He turned, quick as a flash, and caught the tail end of Sharon, whisking herself through the door. Emboldened, he ran after her, cornering her where she couldn't escape, at the top of the stairs that led down to the cloakrooms.

"Well?"

She faced him, brazenly.

"Well what?"

"You never answered my question."

"What question?"

10

"I thought we were supposed to have a date tomorrow?"

"Oh?"

That "oh" maddened him. It really did madden him. Exasperated, he said: "Look, I already told Doug we'd see him down the disco, didn't I?"

"Did you?"

That maddened him even more.

"You know I bloody did!"

Sharon said: "Don't swear. I've told you before."

She was enough to make you swear. He clenched his fists. It was lucky for her he wasn't given to violence. "Look – " He moderated his tone. "Look, when you tell someone you'll do something, you can't just back down at the last minute."

Sharon tossed her head.

"Who's backing down? I don't remember being consulted."

What did she mean, she didn't remember being consulted? Nobody had been consulted. It had just been a general arrangement. She'd been there, she'd been part of it. If she hadn't wanted to come, she should have said so.

"Seems to me," said Sharon, "some people round here take things a bit too much for granted." A blush suddenly appeared on her cheek. He turned his head to discover the cause of it, thinking perhaps it might be the Hubbard, but all he could see was Bob Pearson, coming in from net practice with his hair all sweaty and damp patches on his shirt. Sharon dimpled a smile, shy and almost coy. "Hi, Rob."

Bob Pearson flapped a hand and said: "Hi, Sharon."

So, he knew her name, did he? Second-year sixth,

and knew the name of a fifth-form nobody? Jamie swung back, jealously.

"You needn't think *he*'ll look twice at you."

Already the blush had subsided. With an airy gesture, she slung her bag over her shoulder.

"That's all you know."

He narrowed his eyes.

"Are you going out with him?"

"Might be. Might not be."

She was. He knew that she was. She was jacking him in for that self-satisfied gigolo. That was why she was being pert and unpleasant. She was feeling guilty. Guilt got people that way. As if suddenly repenting, she said: "Sorry about Saturday. You should have asked me earlier. If you're stuck for someone to take, there's always Coral."

Jamie said: "Stuff Coral."

He wasn't so desperate for a bird that they could palm him off with just anybody. Sooner go without. Sooner stay at home and read a book or give a hand humping crates of beer. He wasn't all that crazy about discos, anyway. He wasn't all that crazy about *girls*.

"Perhaps another time," said Sharon.

He felt a strong temptation to say, "Oh, get knotted!" It might not have been particularly intelligent, but it would have given a momentary satisfaction. He wondered, afterwards, why he hadn't.

As he mooched back home, along the wire-netted footpath that bordered the playing fields, he indulged himself in a vision. The scene was the interhouse cricket match, and the vision was of a certain R. Pearson being out for a duck (preferably on the very first ball of the very first over) whilst a certain J. Carr, with cavalier disregard, smote sixes to the right of him and sixes to the left . . . yes, and she needn't think he was going to take her back again, because he wasn't. Not even if she came on her bended knees and begged him. He was through with that little cow. Once and for all, and that was *final*.

2

The day being Friday meant that at eight o'clock he had to stop what he was doing (which on this particular Friday was staring glazed-eyed at the box whilst mentally sticking pins into a waxen image of Sharon) and go over the Common to pick Kim up from her ballet class. It was one of his regular tasks. He'd been doing it for the past three months, ever since she'd got her own way about having two classes a week. Before that, it had just been Saturday mornings, and Saturday mornings she could get there and back under her own steam, because the Common was full of kids and dogs and people taking short cuts, but come the evening it tended to get a bit hairy, what with nutters flashing in the bushes and yobs on motor-cycles frightening the life out of her. She'd come back crying her eyeballs out the first time she'd gone by herself, saying that "some big boys had chased her". Now Jamie had to play escort, at least on the journey home. He didn't really mind. There were some evenings when it could be a drag, like when he had other things to do, but on the whole he preferred it to cleaning the car or humping crates of Guinness. It was Sharon who'd minded. Looking back to last Friday, he realized that that had been the cause of it all – all the flouncing and the head tossing. There'd been a film she wanted to see which started at 7.45. He'd offered to take her on the Saturday, but the Saturday wouldn't do. The Saturday wasn't good enough. It had to be Friday. She'd nagged at him all through the dinner break.

"Why's it have to be you? Why can't someone else go and do it? Why can't your Dad go? It'd only take him five minutes in the car."

When Jamie had said that his father was busy in the shop, she'd said: "Well, your Mum, then! What's wrong with her?"

Jamie had said there wasn't anything wrong with her, except that she couldn't drive.

"Well, so why can't *she* stay in the shop and let *him* go?"

He had shaken his head.

"Not on a Friday. Not by herself."

Sharon had stared at him; as if his mother was daft, or something.

"Why not?"

Patiently, he had tried to explain that running an off-licence wasn't the same as running a news-agent's or confectioner's.

"You get some pretty dodgy customers. Real screwballs. Specially on a Friday." And specially in their part of town. They didn't exactly live in one of the most salubrious areas, tucked away as they were between the flyover and the gasworks, with the Common (the shabby bit, where people dumped their rubbish and scattered Coca Cola tins) strag-gling past the doorstep. "He wouldn't go off and leave her alone. Not unless I was there."

"But it would only take him *five minutes*."

"Yeah – that's if she's on time." Just lately she hadn't been. They were putting on some kind of show for half term, which meant special rehearsals

15

and classes running over. Last week he'd had to kick his heels for almost twenty minutes out on the Common. He'd torn strips off her for that — and Sharon, afterwards, had torn strips off him. She'd sulked all the rest of the evening.

"Why's it have to be *you*?" She'd kept saying it, over and over, as if it were his fault. As if he could have conjured up another member of the family if only he'd been prepared to try hard enough. "Why can't she get the bus, for heaven's sake?"

"Bus only runs once every hour." And in any case, he was getting paid for it. An extra pound a week on his pocket money. He needed that extra pound, he was saving up for a guitar. He was almost half-way there. His mother said it would be a sheer waste of money — "just a craze, like all the others". Like the skateboard and the trumpet. It was perfectly true that the skateboard and the trumpet hadn't lasted very long, but there was a limit to the amount of satisfaction you could get out of a thing like a skateboard, and as for the trumpet, that had been second-hand and half the valves hadn't worked properly. The man in the shop had said it was because it was Chinese. The guitar was going to be different. He was really determined to crack the guitar. Even Sharon had thought it was a good idea — but not if it meant he had to go trailing over the Common at eight o'clock every Friday.

"*Honestly*," she said. "It's *ridiculous*. Anyway, what's she want to do ballet for? Stupid thing to do. Not as if she's ever going to get anywhere. You have to be slim, for ballet. What's she want to go and do it for?"

He hadn't the faintest idea what she wanted to do it for. It didn't seem to him to matter very much *why* she wanted to do it: the important thing was that she *did*. Like he'd wanted to play the trump and now wanted to play the guitar. She could hav picked on something different – swimming, or gym- nastics, or ice skating, or something – but she hadn't, she'd picked on ballet; and if that's what gave her a buzz, wobbling about on her toes and contorting her feet into odd positions, then so what? Why shouldn't she? No call for her Highness to get all snooty about it.

He scowled, as he scuffed his way through the usual litter of Coke tins and Kentucky Fried on to the clear ground beyond. It was typical of Sharon: anything *she* couldn't see the point of, nobody else ought to be able to. As a matter of fact he thought ballet was pretty wet himself, just as he thought art and opera were, but that didn't mean he jeered at people who spent their time walking round art galleries or going to see whatever the name of an opera was. *Madame Butterfly*, or something. *Carmen*, or something. It was a question of what turned you on. Kim was crazy about her ballet. Other kids worshipped footballers and pop stars, but not her. She'd got her bedroom walls all plastered with these photographs – sylph-like females in white skirts pretending to be swans or whatever – and she had this old, grotty ballet shoe she kept wrapped in cotton wool and occasionally took out to show people, so long as they promised not to touch it, and practically not even to *breathe* on it, on account of it had belonged to someone special like Pavlova, except that it wasn't Pavlova, it was some- one he'd never heard of, but anyway someone famous nonetheless. Kim hadn't believed him when he'd said he hadn't heard of her. She'd said he couldn't possibly not have heard of her.

"She was *famous* – she was an asso*luta*."

17

"An asser what?" Jamie had said.

Kim had rolled her eyes.

"Asso*luta*. That means she wasn't just an *ordinary* ballerina – she wasn't even just an ordinary *prima* ballerina – she was a prima ballerina asso*luta*, and *every*body's heard of her – and if they haven't, then they're ignorant as pigs. It's like not having heard of Queen Victoria."

Sometimes, now, when she embarrassed him at bus stops or in the supermarket by suddenly twirling about or sticking her legs out at daft angles, he'd get his own back by saying in a high, squeaky voice "Prima ballerina asso*luta*" so that everyone would turn round to stare and Kim would get all red and self-conscious. For all that, he only ever did it to tease; he never sneered at her. He never said she wouldn't get anywhere. That Sharon could be a right little cow at times.

He walked past the wooded area where the nutters flashed and sometimes hard porn magazines were to be found, on to the chalk pit where the motor-cyclists held their illicit rallies, up to the crest and on to the flat land at the top. This was the better area – Park side, as opposed to Town side. In this area you saw girls in blue velvet riding hats mounted on their own ponies and women in silk scarves walking retrievers. All round the perimeter were large old houses still inhabited by families. (Down in the scrublands any large old house that wasn't derelict was automatically split up into bedsits.)

It was in one of these houses, the one called The Elms, though since Dutch elm disease they'd all been cut down, that Kim's ballet classes were held. There was a board outside which said THEA TUCKER SCHOOL OF DANCE *Director*: *Thea Tucker*. Inside it was just an ordinary house, with a long, dark hallway and a few strategically placed chairs where people like himself could sit and wait when they had to. If it hadn't been for the board outside you wouldn't ever have known that it was supposed to be a school. There was a place in the centre of the town that was far grander. It even sounded grander: it was called the Benton Academy of Dance & Drama, and every year, for the Christmas panto-mime, it provided a troupe of dancers called the Benton Bluebells. Furthermore it taught tap and ballroom as well as ordinary ballet. Thea Tucker only did the classical stuff. He could never under-stand why Kim had insisted on coming to such a one-horse establishment, when she could have gone to something called an Academy. He'd tried asking her, once. He'd said: "There's a girl in my class goes to the Benton Academy – " It was as far as he'd got. Kim had instantly screwed up her face, with its absurd button nose, and said: "*That* place!" She'd managed to pack more scorn into the words than you'd have thought a twelve-year-old with a button nose was capable of. He hadn't said anything more after that.

This evening when he pushed open the heavy front door, which was always left on the latch during class times, the hallway was empty. Had the class ended when it should, there would have been a stream of small girls rushing up the stairs in their practice costumes, or down again with bags full of ballet shoes, all changed and ready to go. Instead, from behind a closed door further down the passage, he heard the tinkling of a piano, accompanied by a rhythmic clopping and thumping which he had learnt to recognize as the sound of feet in what Kim called "blocked shoes". He clicked his tongue,

19

irritably – more to convince himself that he *was* irritated than because he actually was. He didn't really object to wandering about the Common for another thirty minutes. In fact, he quite enjoyed looking at all the rich people going in and out of their rich houses. It was the principle of the thing rather than the thing itself. If the brat thought she could keep him hanging around like this every week, then she had another think coming. Unless, of course, he were to charge *waiting* time?

The door at the far end of the passage had opened and a girl had come out. She looked at him and said: "Have you come to collect someone?"

She was the sort of girl who always made him tongue-tied. She obviously belonged to rich people, because her voice was what a young Kim had once called "lardy dardy", really meaning Laurel and Hardy, only now they tended to use it for anything that was at all posh. "Oh, very lardy dardy," his Dad would say, when Mum got done up in her best for family occasions. He would have said it now, looking at this girl. She was dressed in a black leotard thing and tights, with blonde hair (the silver kind, not yellowy) pulled straight back into a bun, the way Kim was always trying to do hers except that it hadn't yet grown long enough, and even when it had it wouldn't suit her, because Kim had this little round squashy face like a currant bun. The girl who had appeared at the far end of the passage was all thin and sculpted. She might have stepped straight out of one of Kim's ballet photos. She said again: "Have you come for someone?"

Jamie found his tongue.

"My sister – Kim Carr."

"They're just running something through. I should think they'll be about another ten minutes."

"Oh. Well, in that case – " He snatched at the front door. "I'll come back."

"You can wait inside if you'd like."

"No. That's all right." He'd rather be out on the Common than shut up here with nothing to look at but a pile of ballet magazines.

"The thing is," said the girl, "they might be longer than ten minutes – they might be half an hour. They're doing their Dewdrop routine." She paused, looking at him. "Why don't you come along and watch?"

Come along and watch? *Him?* Watch a pack of small girls doing a Dewdrop routine? She must be joking!

"They wouldn't want me in there," he said.

That was a mistake: he realized it the minute he'd said it. He should have told her he had other things to do. Now he'd laid himself wide open.

"Actually," said the girl, "it would do them good to have someone there. It would give them an audience – someone to play to. Give them an incentive to get things right."

He muttered: "I wouldn't know if they got things right or if they didn't," but he'd left himself without a leg to stand on. The girl said seriously: "Ah, but they're not to know that, are they? Do come! I'm sure you'll like it."

It seemed he had no alternative. Limp with embarrassment, he shambled down the passage; sheepishly, as she flung open the door, he slunk in at her heels.

"Take a seat."

She waved him into a chair. He slumped down on to it, legs flung out before him, arms folded across his chest, trying to look as if he couldn't care less, which in the circumstances wasn't that easy. He'd

21

never been alone in a whole roomful of females before, especially half-naked ones; and just to add to his discomfiture, when at last he felt strong enough to risk a quick glance he found that the room was surrounded on three of its sides by full-length mirrors, which meant that you could hardly help staring at yourself whether you wanted to or not.

He shuffled on his seat, and his reflection shuffled with him. It looked stern, and ill at ease; shabby, too, in washed-up jeans and an old blue sweat shirt with UNIVERSITY OF ILLINOIS printed across the chest. He wondered what on earth had possessed him to get a sweat shirt with UNIVERSITY OF ILLINOIS splashed all over it. For crying out loud, he didn't even know that Illinois *had* a university.

The clopping and the thudding was still going on. Clop-*thud*. Clop-*thud*. At close range it sounded like a herd of three-legged buffaloes. He raised his eyes a fraction, and the buffaloes turned into a dozen small girls in pink tunics all leaping about in a circle. Some of them were looking solemn, and some of them were wearing bright, fixed, toothy grins, but each and every one had her arms held up in the air and her head tilted to one side, making like mad to be dewdrops. Kim was making like mad along with the rest. The circle dissolved and then re-formed itself into a line, and there was Kim, bang in the middle, all beaming and porky with her fingers splayed out stiff and straight with the effort she was putting into it. Good old Kim! Even he could see that her fingers weren't *supposed* to be all stiff and straight. Not if it was a dewdrop she was being. Maybe if it had been a streak of lightning or an icicle or something; but not a dewdrop. He wished there were some way of getting it across to her: "Relax those fingers!" It was what Mr Butterworth was always bellowing at them in the gym, only with him it was shoulders – *"Relax those shoulders!"*, accompanied by a vicious chopping up and down with both hands that left you sore for days afterwards.

The girl who was responsible for his being there had gone across to the piano and was talking earnestly – he could tell that it was earnestly, from her expression – to an elderly lady who he supposed must be the famous Thea Tucker that Kim was always on about. For months past it had been "Miss Tucker says this" and "Miss Tucker says that". She had become almost a household god.

He gazed at her, covertly, through the mirror. At first glance she didn't seem anything particularly special. She must have been at least as old as his Dad's mother, yet she was plastered in make-up and wearing a black pleated knee-length skirt over a boat-necked leotard and flesh-coloured tights. It was a get-up which would have looked positively ridiculous, not to say downright indecent, if his Gran had tried wearing it – positively ridiculous if his *mother* had tried. On Miss Tucker it somehow looked OK, perhaps because she hadn't gone shapeless like most old people. Her face was all wrinkled, he could see that even at this distance, and the veins on her neck were knotted like cords, but the rest of her might almost have passed for a young girl.

She suddenly glanced across at him, and he looked away, confused. Were they talking about him? Out of the corner of his eye he saw the girl nod in his direction. He saw Miss Tucker frown. It was a frown that contained more of doubt than of active disapproval, but all the same he felt himself grow hot.

What were they talking about? Why did they keep looking at him like that? What was supposed to be the matter with him?

Self-consciously, he sat up straighter on his chair. He unfolded his arms, tried crossing his legs, found the washed-out jeans had grown too tight, and hastily uncrossed them. Miss Tucker and the girl stood watching his antics judiciously, as if he were giving a performance for which he was to be awarded marks out of ten. He half turned, on his chair, so that they only had him in profile. In front of him, the Dewdrops thundered to a halt, more or less in time with the music. Miss Tucker detached herself from the piano and moved forward into the room. She walked with a strange, duck-like waddle, her feet splayed out at right angles. It should have looked graceless, but in fact it didn't: she had too much regality about her for that.

"All right, children!" She clapped her hands. "That was better than last time, but do try to remember that you're meant to be dewdrops. Not cart-horses ... Kim, dear, watch those fingers. They look like bunches of twigs. Deirdre, remind me I want to take a look at your ankles sometime. Andrea – yes." Her lips tightened. "Andrea I shall have a Word with tomorrow."

At this, an exceptionally tiny child with a cheeky elfin face grew very pink and looked as if she might be about to burst into tears. Jamie felt sorry for her. He wondered what terrible crime she had committed. Later, when he asked Kim about it Kim went all big-eyed and said: "She forgot her belt ... her elastic belt, you know. To wear round her tunic. *And* she did it last week. Miss Tucker was *furious*."

Miss Tucker, now, having bestowed upon the

unfortunate Andrea a look which would have quelled a lump of granite, said: "Very well, then. Off you go. Ten o'clock sharp in the morning – we'll take it straight through to Anita's solo."

All the little pink Dewdrops chorused: "Yes, Miss Tucker. Good night, Miss Tucker", bobbed themselves up and down like corks on a high sea as they curtsied (why did they do that, Jamie wondered? She wasn't royalty) and went clip-clopping off towards the door. The girl, he noticed, had already gone. He made to follow, and found himself detained by Miss Tucker. She said: "Anita tells me that you're Kim's brother."

Anita. So that was her name – and they *had* been talking about him. He knew that they must have been. Now he supposed he was going to be told off for being there. He opened his mouth to defend himself, but before he could say anything Miss Tucker, abruptly, had said: "Are you musical?"

"Musical?" The question took him by surprise. He considered it a moment. He had once sung in the church choir, when he was too young to know any better, and Miss Hargreaves at school had never actually asked him to shut up or told him that he must be tone deaf, as she had Doug. On the other hand, discretion was always the better part of vainglory. After all, why did she want to know? Cautiously, not committing himself, he said: "Not specially."

'You don't play anything?"

He thought of the second-hand trumpet, and the guitar, and said: "No." And then, as an afterthought, in case that sounded ungracious: "Kim does." Kim had had piano lessons once a week until she'd started clamouring for ballet instead. The family couldn't afford both – that was why Jamie had never learnt. It was music and ballet for Kim, football and cricket for Jamie. Just as well, really. He wouldn't have wanted to spend hours thumping about on a piano. He wouldn't have minded a bit of encouragement over that trumpet, though. He bet with a bit of encouragement he could have learnt how to play it. As it was, every time he'd tried putting it to his lips his mother had complained of a headache and his father had said: "If you blow that down my ear once more I'll confiscate the perishing thing." They'd never made all that fuss about Kim and her piano, even though it had lived in the same room as the television set. Still, he didn't mind giving her a plug, if it was likely to raise her stock with the formidable Miss Tucker. "Kim can play pretty well," he said. "She did it for two years. She passed these exams."

Miss Tucker didn't seem very interested in Kim or her exams. She only went on looking at Jamie, and said: "What about your sense of rhythm? Do you have a sense of rhythm?"

He shrugged a shoulder. How should he know? It wasn't something he'd ever given any thought to. Miss Tucker grew impatient.

"Can you move in time to music? If you hear a piece of music – Marjorie!" She turned, with a peremptory snap of the fingers, to the little mouse lady who had been playing the piano. "Give him something to move about to."

The little mouse lady, who had been on her way out through the door, obediently turned and pattered back again. She sat herself down, opened the lid of the piano and began to play. He wondered if she'd charge overtime, or if she didn't mind being exploited.

"There you are." Miss Tucker jerked her head. "See what you can do."

He stared at her, bemused.

"Well, go along," she said; and she shooshed at him with her hands as if he were a chicken. "Go and do something."

Reluctantly, he shuffled a few paces forward.

"Do what?"

"Whatever you feel inspired to do." (Cut and run. This place was a mad house. The woman herself was obviously a raving lunatic.) "Just move about, in time to the music."

Feeling the biggest idiot this side of the moon, he slouched pigeon-toed across the room. Her voice called imperiously after him: "Come along, come along, young man! You can do better than that! Listen to the music – what is it telling you? It's telling you to *move*, isn't it? Well, then ... move! Let's see some action. *Yum*-pum, *yum*-pum, *yum*-pum, put some animation into it! Lift up those feet! Shake out those shoulders! Good gracious me, anyone would think you were suffering from sleeping sickness ... you haven't got anything wrong with you, have you?"

He was nettled. Did he look as if he had?

"If this is the way you carry on when you go to discos – "

"It's not the way I carry on when I go to discos!" Goaded, he turned on her. "It's different at discos."

"How?" said Miss Tucker. "In what way is it different?"

The music was different – everything was different. For one thing, you had a bird.

"For one thing," he said, "you have a – " The word died on his lips. "You have a partner," he said.

27

"Oh! So that's what's bothering you. Well, that's easily remedied."

Before he knew what she intended, Miss Tucker had come waltzing out into the middle of the room. Gaily, she seized him by the hand.

"There we are, then . . . let's get with it!"

3

It ought by rights to have been the most embarrassing thing that had ever happened to him – disco dancing to the wrong sort of music with a daft old bat as old as his grandmother. Oddly enough, it wasn't. He was even managing, reluctantly, by the end, to get some sort of a kick out of it. He was pretty sure Miss Tucker was, too, the way she was flinging herself about. Really, you had to hand it to her: she might be a daft old bat, but she'd certainly got spirit. Her enthusiasm was such that it would have made him look even sillier standing on his dignity than stepping down and joining in. He was glad, all the same, that Doug wasn't there.

"Well!" said Miss Tucker. She was hardly any more out of breath than he was. "That was something different."

She could say that again. He wondered, now, if she would let him go. He began sidling towards the door, but before he could get there it had opened and the girl, Anita, had reappeared. She had changed out of her black leotard into T-shirt and jeans, with her hair pulled back into an ordinary elastic band, but still you could tell that she belonged to rich people. She had that sort of an air about her. As soon as she saw Jamie she said: "Has he agreed to – "at the same moment as Miss Tucker said: "Do you know, I really think he'll do?"

Do? He froze. Do for what? What was this? Some kind of a set-up?

Miss Tucker, taking him by the arm, said: "Come over here and stand by Anita."

He didn't know why he let himself be pushed around like this, he really didn't. She had absolutely no right – *he* wasn't one of her pupils. The habit of obedience was too strong, that was the trouble. Meekly, he allowed himself to be ranged by the side of the girl. She'd looked tall, at first, on account of she was so skinny, but in fact she didn't come much above his shoulder. Miss Tucker measured them both with her eye.

"Yes," she said. "The match is perfect. Heightwise he couldn't be better." Better? For *what*? "And I must say he is excellently proportioned." By now, the girl was also measuring him with her eye. They stood before him, the pair of them, critically raking him up and down. He began to feel uncomfortable, like a prize bull in the market place. Perhaps they were white-slave traders, shipping young men off to distant parts for nefarious purposes. Doug said things went on in some countries you'd never believe. Perhaps they ran a *brothel*.

"Do you do a lot of athletics?" said Miss Tucker.

Defiantly, he said: "Yes." He didn't know why he said it defiantly, except that it sounded better that way. Miss Tucker nodded.

"I thought you must do – swimming, probably." She squeezed at his upper arm. "That's why your muscles are so well developed."

He didn't bother telling her that the reason his muscles were developed was because he'd spent the last few years humping crates of booze up from the cellar.

"Well, now," said Miss Tucker. He stiffened. Here it came. The moment of truth. "How would you feel about helping us out?"

He looked at her, guardedly. Not with any brothel, he didn't help out. If they wanted a strong-arm guy, they could look elsewhere. Doug, for instance. It was the sort of thing that Doug would probably enjoy.

"Do say you will!" Anita was looking at him beseechingly, both hands clasped to her bosom (what there was of it). "The show's going on in six weeks."

"Show?"

"Yes! We're getting absolutely desperate."

"What we need," said Miss Tucker, "is a man."

"Oh – " He relaxed. So that was all they wanted him for: the show. Presumably to shift scenery, or something. He said: "We-e-ll – " He supposed he wouldn't actually mind. Lugging bits of scenery about would be as nothing besides hefting those everlasting crates up the cellar steps, and it wasn't as if he had much else on just at present. Not now that he'd finally chucked Sharon. On the other hand –

"You wouldn't have to *do* much," said Anita. "Only just *be* there. You'd never believe how difficult men are to come by."

Miss Tucker explained.

"Our only really *mature* young man, unfortunately, broke his arm last week in a motor-cycle accident. I warned him time and again, such machines are lethal, but of course he wouldn't listen. Now he's in a plaster cast and quite useless."

"All we're left with are kids," said Anita. "And, of course" (a note of scorn crept into her voice), "and, of course, *Garstin*."

Miss Tucker sighed.

"Poor Garstin. He does try. But I'm afraid that no amount of trying will compensate for lack of physique."

"Not to mention being able to keep time to the music," said Anita. She said it with a certain bitterness.

"Oh!" Miss Tucker beamed. She laid a hand on Jamie's head. "Kim's brother has an excellent sense of timing! He is naturally rhythmical. I have already made sure of *that*."

Jamie was growing uncomfortable again. What was all this about "naturally rhythmical"? They weren't expecting him to shift scenery in time to *Swan Lake*, were they? He looked suspiciously from one to the other of them; from Anita, whose eyes, he saw with surprise, were actually green – not blue-green, or grey-green, but real greeny-green – to Miss Tucker, who was studying him again in that way he didn't like, the white-slave way, taking in all the details.

"Yes," she said. "One must have the physique. Without it, one has no bearing. I'm afraid poor Garstin is rather like a beanpole. I knew that it would happen. He's shot up too fast – outrun his strength. Not that it would make a great deal of difference if he hadn't. If one isn't musical, one isn't musical, and that's about all there is to it."

"Look," said Jamie. He cleared a frog out of his throat. "What exactly – "

"If I've got to dance with Garstin," said Anita, "then I'd rather not dance at all."

Dance? *Dance?* The message, suddenly, got through. He backed away, indignantly. *Him? Dance?* Oh, no! No, no! They weren't getting him on that lark. No way. Not a chance.

"Actually," he said, "I'm pretty busy just at the moment." He had exams the end of this term. One "O" and some CSEs. They couldn't expect him to mess about on some tinpot little show. Anyway, *him*?

"It's not as if we should want you here every night," said Miss Tucker. "Only just now and again, and occasionally for a private session with Anita."

In other circumstances he might not have objected to a few private sessions with Anita – he wouldn't have minded going to the cinema with her, for example. He wouldn't have minded taking her to the disco. He wondered if she was the sort of girl who went to discos. Probably not. Probably considered it not cultural enough. He bet she'd rather go to the opera or an art gallery.

"You needn't worry that we'd want you to do anything complex," said Miss Tucker. "There are only a couple of small lifts involved. I'm sure you wouldn't have any difficulty with those – I'm sure you could lift Anita with no trouble at all."

Lift her? He could throw her about like a sack of coals, if that was what they wanted. There was hardly anything of her, she couldn't weigh more than about six stone. But anyhow, the question wouldn't arise because he wasn't going to do it.

"Naturally, if they were too much for you," said Miss Tucker, "we should have to modify them. But I don't foresee any difficulty. Not with that physique." He squirmed. "And then, of course" – she spoke briskly – "one has to consider the presentation aspect. It's a distinct advantage, your being so dark – seeing as Anita is so fair. It will make a good strong contrast."

"And after all, it is for a *cause*," said Anita.

"Oh, yes. We always support a Cause. Last year it

33

was Save the Children, this year it's Spastics." Miss Tucker shot Jamie a shrewd glance. "Didn't Kim say you had a little cousin who was a spastic?"

He glowered. Trust Kim. She *would* have to go shooting her mouth off, wouldn't she? He mumbled, grudgingly.

"What?" said Miss Tucker. "Speak up, young man, and don't swallow your words!"

"I said yes," said Jamie. "She goes to Fairfield."

"*Fair*field." A look of triumph settled itself on Miss Tucker's face. "The very institution to whom we are giving the proceeds!"

He felt himself becoming trapped. Anita, quite obviously, had already decided that that was that – there could be no further grounds for argument. Fairfield had clinched it, as far as she was concerned.

"Well, there you are, then!" She turned, excitedly, to Miss Tucker – "It means we could put the Russian dance back in!" – spun round again, to Jamie – "*You* could do a Russian dance, couldn't you?"

He said stolidly: "Russian dance?"

"Yes! You know! Like the Red Army do – like the Cossacks – like this!"

All of a sudden she was down on her haunches with her arms folded across her chest, flinging her legs out. He had to admit that it looked pretty good – but he was willing to bet it was quite easy. He daresay he could do it, if he really felt inclined. He was almost impelled to get down there with her and try it, but before he could be betrayed into any such display of weakness he had intercepted a warning frown from Miss Tucker to Anita. He knew very well what the frown meant. He wasn't an idiot. It meant, we've nearly got him, don't frighten him off

34

. . . one thing at a time: let's get the fish hooked
first . . .

That did it. He hardened his resolve.

"I reckon I ought to be going," he said. "Kim'll be
waiting for me."

"But you will agree to do it," said Anita, "won't
you? *Please!*"

"Let him think about it," said Miss Tucker.

He seized at the suggestion, gratefully.

"Yeah," he said. "I'll think about it." He wrenched
open the door. "I'll let you know."

The only reason he couldn't let them know there
and then was that he was too much of a coward. He
couldn't tell them, straight out, I wouldn't be caught
dead dancing in your crummy little show. He'd get
Kim to do it for him tomorrow. On second thoughts,
he wouldn't get Kim to do it for him tomorrow. He'd
rather Kim didn't know anything about it, she'd
only start nagging at him. He could just hear her.
"But, Jamie, it's for *spastics*." Perhaps it would be
easier if he simply let it slip his mind. Simply forgot
about it.

Accordingly, he did so – but not before he'd spent
ten minutes in his bedroom having a go at the
Cossack thing. Just out of interest, that was all.
Just to see if he could do it. (He could, but his
mother didn't like it. She yelled at him up the stairs
to "Stop that, whatever it is you're doing! You'll
have the ceiling down!") After that, he didn't think
of it any more.

On Saturday evening, for want of anything more
intelligent to do (he didn't really feel like going
down to the disco by himself, and in any case he
might bump into Sharon mooning over Bob Pearson,
and that would just about finish him) he was sitting
slumped before the box with the rest of the family

when the telephone rang and it was for him. His mother came back from the hall and said: "Jamie, there's a young lady wants you." He'd known at once that it couldn't be Sharon. Sharon had never been "a young lady". She'd only been "that Sharon".

"Talks very nicely," said his mother. "Asked if she could have a word with you."

It was, of course, Anita. He might have known she wouldn't give up that easily. She said: "Hallo! Is that Kim's brother? I do hope you don't mind me ringing, but I've been on tenterhooks all day. I knew if I didn't find out I'd never be able to settle to anything ... *are* you going to be able to help us? With the show?"

He was a fool. A dolt. A clod. A weak-kneed, lily-livered, yellow-bellied *clod*. Why couldn't he have said no, very firmly, right at the outset? Why couldn't he say no, very firmly, right now?

Because he was a clod, that was why.

He said: "Well – "

"We'd really be most *terribly* grateful," said Anita. 'Oh, I do hope you can! I simply don't know what we'll do if you can't."

By the time he went back to the box, he had committed himself.

4

"The square of the sum on the hypotenuse – " Jamie
floundered, came to a halt, tried again. "The *sum* of
the squares on the hypotenuse – "

"Yes?"

"In a right-angled triangle – "

"Yes?"

He took a breath.

"In – a – right – angled – triangle – the – sum –
of – the – squares – on – the – hypotenuse – is –
equal – to – the – sum – of – the – squares – on –
the – other – two – sides."

"Oh!" said Mr Hubbard. "It is, is it?"

No; obviously it wasn't. It had obviously gone
wrong somewhere. It was all a load of blithering
rubbish, anyway. Mr Hubbard regarded him with
interest.

"How many squares, exactly, were you proposing
to have on this hypotenuse of yours?"

"Er – two?" said Jamie.

"Two?"

"Well – " He shrugged. It seemed as good a
number as any.

Doug, in his rough book, wrote: ARSEOLES.

"I suppose you do know what the hypotenuse is?"
mused Mr Hubbard.

Now that he came to mention it, he wasn't at all

sure that he did. As far as he was concerned, it was just a thing that was found in right-angled triangles – a thing which for some reason he couldn't fathom had squares attached to it, which squares, for another reason he couldn't fathom, were held to be equal to certain other squares also to be found in right-angled triangles. And what the use of it was was more than he could say. He wondered if the Queen would know, if someone were to ask her. If someone were to go up to her and say, "Excuse me, your Queen, but do you know what the hypotenuse is – "

"*Well?*" said Mr Hubbard.

The creep was actually expecting a reply.

"Well," said Jamie. Sharon turned her head to look at him. "Well," he said, "it's – it's something you get in a right-angled triangle."

Oh, ha ha. Very funny. Titter titter. What a joke. Sharon had turned back again, her shoulders shaking. He scowled. He bet *she* couldn't get down on her haunches and kick her legs out. Couldn't even run for a bus, that one, without tripping over her own feet. Couldn't even dive two inches off the side of the pool without doing a belly flop.

He became aware that Mr Hubbard was studying him. His face wore an air of puzzled wonderment, as if he were gazing upon some new species of earthworm hitherto unknown to man.

"Tell me, laddie – " He leaned forward, across the desk, towards him. "Is it that you are bone idle, or are you just naturally thick?"

"One, two – *up* – hold – balance her with the right hand – round, three, four – down, gently – good – pause for the arabesque – two, three – now, give her your left hand – *left!* – good – lead her forward –

38

three, four – pause – prepare to support – yes, that's good! That's good! That's excellent!"

At least there was *some*thing he could do right. Old Miss Tucker was as bucked as if he'd just scaled the north face of the Eiger. All he'd done was lift some strip of a girl up into the air and then put her back down again so that she could use him as a balancing post while she stood on one leg. He was glad that they were happy (remembering the incident of the small girl and the missing elastic belt he thought that taken all in all he would rather face the scorn of a Mr Hubbard than the wrath of a Miss Tucker) but still he couldn't really see that he'd done anything so wonderful. He obviously had, however. Old Miss Tucker was beaming away like mad, and Anita had both her hands clasped to what passed for her bosom.

"Jamie," she said, "that was great! It really was!"

He grinned, in spite of himself. It hadn't felt too bad to him, either. In fact, if he was to be honest, he'd got quite a kick out of it. For all she was so skinny she hadn't felt bony, as he'd half expected. Instead, she'd been quite firm and warm, like next door's terrier, which might be tiny but was nevertheless all muscle. (Unlike his Gran's King Charles, which was just a lump of yielding flesh into which your fingers, unpleasantly, sank fathoms deep as you tried to lift it.)

"It would seem," said Miss Tucker, still beaming, "that you have a natural instinct."

"*Honestly*," said Anita, "it felt as if we'd been working together for *weeks*."

Even now he couldn't think what they were making all the fuss about. He tried to feel pleased with himself, but how could you bask when you still didn't know what you were supposed to have done? Miss Tucker attempted to enlighten.

"The art of partnering is not as easy as you obviously think. It is not simply a question of being on hand at the right moment – anyone can be taught to do that."

("Anyone except Garstin," muttered Anita.)

"What *cannot* be taught is the ability to work in harmony. For that one needs a degree of mutual sympathy which is either there or not there. Fortunately, in your case" – the beam returned – "it evidently is."

Well, if that was what she chose to believe. He couldn't say he'd noticed himself feeling in any particular sympathy with Anita. Not that he felt *out* of sympathy. She was pleasant enough, and at least she didn't have that maddening female habit of giggling. He hated it when they giggled. It always seemed to him that they were doing it on purpose to create feelings of insecurity. Anita certainly wasn't guilty of that; but even so – even discounting the fact that she belonged to rich people and that he didn't – it was difficult to see what they could ever have in common to feel sympathy about.

"It has always been my contention," said Miss Tucker, "that great partnerships are born, and not made. You have only to look at Markova and Dolin – "

"Or Fonteyn and Nureyev," said Anita.

"Or Fonteyn and Nureyev," said Miss Tucker.

Jamie wanted to say, "Or Hobbs and Sutcliffe?" but thought perhaps it might not be appropriate. Miss Tucker and Anita probably wouldn't know who they were – worse still, might not even have heard of them. Come to that, he'd never heard of Markova and Dolin. He'd heard of Margot Fonteyn, of course, because everybody had, and he'd heard of Rudolph Nureyev till he was sick of the very sound of him. Rudolph Nureyev was one of Kim's idols, coming second only to the prima ballerina assoluta of the shoe. Sometimes, when he felt that she deserved taking down a peg, he'd rib her about it and ask "How's the old Red-Nosed Reindeer, then?" It never failed to make her mad.

"You know – " Miss Tucker was giving him the old slave-trader look again, through half-closed eyes with her head to one side. "You know, I cannot help feeling that you should be doing something on your own account. Something simple, but spectacular – "

"David's solo!" cried Anita. "He could do David's solo!"

Jamie stared at her in alarm. He hadn't agreed to do anyone's solos: he had only agreed to act as forklift truck and balancing post. They weren't getting him out there all by himself.

"Mm . . ." Miss Tucker sounded thoughtful. "Possibly if we were to scale it down – "

"It's not as if there's anything madly technical. Only right at the end."

"Yes, we couldn't expect him to manage fouettés."

Instantly, he wondered why not. (He asked Kim, later: "What's a fouetté?" Kim said: "It's what Odile does in *Swan Lake* . . . she does *thirty-two*, and all on the same spot." "Yes," said Jamie, "but what *are* they?" "Well – " Kim wrinkled her button nose. "They're a sort of turning thing, when you whip one leg round the other." "Show." "I can't," said Kim, and she giggled. "I fall over . . .")

"Let me think," said Miss Tucker. "Can you jump?"

Could he jump? Once won medals for it, hadn't he? He said so – rather more boastfully, perhaps, than he had intended. Anita immediately said: "Long jump, or high jump?" Pride carried him away.

"Both," he said, carelessly. One year it had been one, one year it had been the other. "I'm OK at either."

"Yes, but not in those trousers." Miss Tucker suddenly bent down and twitched at the leg of his jeans. "Ridiculous! It's a wonder you can move at all. Remind me, for next time, to look out some tights for you."

His blood ran cold. He saw himself, through the medium of the obtrusive mirrors, backing away in something like panic. *Tights?*

"You'll find them much more comfortable. Far less restricting. Nobody can dance in skin-tight jeans."

Desperately, he said: "I've got some others at home. These have shrunk a bit. The others aren't so tight."

"They'll still be too tight to dance in. Look at you! Can't even bend your legs properly."

"Yes, I can," he said.

"Nonsense! Of course you can't."

"I can!"

Miss Tucker gave him a look: it was the sort of look she had given the small girl, Andrea.

"I have been in this business," she said, "for almost forty years. I have taught Household Names. I know what I am talking about."

There was a silence. Anita, diplomatically, studied her nails.

"What is your objection," said Miss Tucker, "to wearing tights? Is there something wrong with your legs? Or are you simply prejudiced?" His cheeks flared: he mumbled, inarticulately. "Simply prejudiced," said Miss Tucker. "How sad! I thought modern youth had grown out of that sort of thing. I thought you were more liberated. Evidently not. Well, in that case, all the more reason why you should start wearing them now. It will give you a chance to get used to them by the time of the performance." His horror must have shown in his face. "My dear boy," said Miss Tucker, "you surely didn't think you were going to be allowed to *perform* in jeans?"

He walked part of the way home with Anita, who lived in one of the big new houses that bordered the golf course, over on the south side of the Common. She obviously felt him to be in need of comfort and reassurance, for suddenly, in the middle of a silence, when he had been wondering what he ought to talk about, she said: "Did you know that soldiers in the British Army sometimes wear tights?"

He looked at her, sideways.

"Oh, yes? Special issue, I suppose . . . for when they do *Swan Lake*."

"No." She rode his sarcasm quite calmly. "Not special issue, just ordinary women's tights. And not for when they do *Swan Lake*: for when they're going off on route marches and the temperature's sub-zero . . . I know you don't believe me, but it's perfectly true. My uncle told me. He said there's nothing to beat a pair of tights for keeping out the cold. And he ought to know," she added. "He's been up Everest in them."

He felt like saying: "I've got this uncle goes in for ladies' stockings . . . wears 'em over his head every time he does a bank job." It was the sort of thing that Doug would have said. Instead, he only humped a shoulder and made a grumping noise. Everest was one thing: disporting yourself on stage before a gaping crowd of people was another.

"But in any case," said Anita, kindly, "I shouldn't

worry too much if I were you . . . you'll have a nice long tunic to go over the top."

He wasn't sure whether she was teasing him or not. Her voice was serious enough, but he thought he caught a hint of laughter in the green eyes. He grunted, and said nothing. They'd just better think themselves lucky if he deigned to turn up next week, that was all.

The interhouse cricket match was a farce. He was sent in at number three and he made three runs and dropped about the same number of catches (two of which would admittedly have been pretty spectacular in anyone's book, but for one of which there was simply no excuse) and altogether made about as big an exhibition of himself as even Sharon could have wished. She came up to him afterwards and said: "That was rotten luck, getting run out like that." He wondered if she were gloating, or if she really meant it. Probably gloating. Probably only too glad to see him humiliated. She was still making goo-goo eyes at Bob Pearson, great self-important oaf that he was, strutting up and down in his First Eleven pullover, with his cap jammed over his eyes, making like he was W. G. Grace and Don Bradman and Len Hutton all rolled into one. Jamie shrugged a shoulder and said, "Oh, it happens" – lofty, offhand, couldn't-care-less – and slunk away to nurse his grievances in private.

It hadn't been all his fault. The one catch that he'd muffed, that had been his fault; but not the running out. That had been the Pearson, that had. Selfish great lout – talk about hogging all the bowling. No one else had had a look in. From the moment Jamie had joined him at the wicket it had been nothing but a constant stream of orders bawled down the pitch – "*Now*, partner!" "Come *along*, partner!" "You can *make* it, partner!" – with Jamie tearing to and fro like a stuck pig from one set of stumps to the other and him bagging all the honour and glory and knocking up all the runs. Thirty-nine not out, *he*'d ended up with (out of a paltry total of sixty-nine). Jamie had managed to scrape three, off a short ball at the end of an over, which would have left him facing the bowling. Mister Pearson hadn't liked that. He'd yelled: "Yes, yes, and another one, partner!" And then, too late, on a note of panic: "No, get back! Get back!"

Abandoned between wickets, Jamie hadn't stood a chance. He'd had no alternative but to turn and make a mad dash, in a despairing attempt to get his bat over the crease before a well-flung return sent the bails flying. Only inches from safety, he'd fallen flat on his face. He never wanted to think of it again. Never as long as he lived. From now on he wouldn't even bother to make his ritual detour through the Assembly Hall on a Friday afternoon and throw his casual glance at the notice board. He wouldn't even go through the actions. There wouldn't be any point; not after this.

Doug, next day, as they slouched round the field together during the morning break, said: "That cretin. Deserves to be shot, getting you run out like that." The sore patch in Jamie's heart became at this just a tiny bit less sore. If Doug had noticed, then surely others must have done? "Guy's an idiot," said Doug. "Know what you want to do, next time he tries it . . . dig in your heels, and just don't move. That's what I'd do."

Jamie kicked glumly at an empty Coca Cola can. "Don't s'pose there'll be any next time."

"Course there will," said Doug. "You weren't given

a fair chance. Everybody's got to be given a fair chance. Stands to reason."

Nevertheless, his name wasn't there when he walked past the notice board on the following Friday. He'd known that it wouldn't be; but still, the injustice smarted.

He had been hoping against hope that Miss Tucker would have forgotten her threat of finding him a pair of tights to wear, but of course she hadn't. He had known that she wouldn't, just as he'd known his name wouldn't be on the notice board; but if the injustice of the one continued to rankle, the embarrassment of the other very nearly annihilated. It wasn't so much what it *looked* like – he wasn't knock-kneed, or anything; he wasn't bandy-legged – as what it *felt* like. What it felt like was walking about naked, almost. He didn't know how people could. Not unless they were exhibitionists, which he was not, in spite of falling flat on his face in front of half the school: not unless they actually *enjoyed* being stared at and pointed at and sniggered about. He felt an absolute idiot, and just to make matters worse she'd gone and given him these stupid shoes. He'd been wearing trainers up till now. He didn't see how she could complain about trainers. If you could run in them, there wasn't any reason why you couldn't dance in them – except that he wasn't going to be doing any dancing. He'd come to a firm decision on that point. He was going to make it very clear. He'd agreed to help Anita do *her* bits and pieces: he hadn't agreed to do any on his own account. And furthermore, if there were any snide remarks on the subject of *tights* –

There weren't. When he entered the room, scowling to cover up his discomfiture at being seen abroad in such absurd and inadequate attire, Anita was already there, doing knee-bends at the rails (*"Pliés,"* she said, later. "And it's a barre, not a rail") while Miss Tucker was conferring at the piano with the little mouse lady, whose name was Miss Harrell. At the sound of the door, they all glanced up. Anita waved a casual hand and went on with her exercises; Miss Harrell smiled and nodded; Miss Tucker said: "Good boy! You're on time." Nobody gave any signs of thinking he looked odd or peculiar. The only reference made to his change of costume was by Miss Tucker, who said: "Well! Now that you're dressed properly, we can get you doing things."

He tried his best to explain that he didn't want to do things – that *doing* things had been no part of his agreement. Miss Tucker, impatient, brushed all objections to one side.

"Don't be so silly, of course you want to do things. What's the matter with you? You're not shy, are you? You shouldn't be, looking like that. You should be only too happy to show yourself off. A little bit of healthy exhibitionism never hurt anyone. That's what a solo's designed for, you know. After all" – she said it briskly, as if there could be no possible doubt in the matter – "you don't just want to be a clothes prop, do you? Of course you don't. That would be very poor-spirited. Now, when you've led Anita off, what I want you to do is to come back on – can we have the music, Marjorie? – with a series of grands jetés right around the stage – what are you puckering your forehead for? I suppose you don't know what a grand jeté is? Well, that's soon remedied. It's nothing in the least alarming. Just a rather spectacular kind of jump. But perfectly simple . . . Anita, dear, could you show?'

Anita obligingly peeled herself up from the floor,

where she'd been sitting slumped against the wall in a crumpled lotus position, and before Jamie's helpless gaze took off across the room in a series of flying leaps.

"There, now," said Miss Tucker. She beamed at him, triumphantly. "With all those medals for jumping? Don't tell me you can't do *that*."

"Want to see something?" said Doug.

"Not particularly."

They were sitting out on the field, where Jamie was struggling to get Doug's maths homework copied into his own book before it was time to go and face the Hubbard for another session of public scourging and humiliation. Not that Doug's maths was any more sparkling than his, but a page full of rubbish was a safer bet than a page full of nothing at all. In any case, when Doug said: "Want to see something?" it usually meant something pornographic that he'd picked up on the Common. Jamie could live without it. It certainly wouldn't break his heart.

"Get away!" Doug nudged at him. "Do you good." He took a quick look to make sure there were no staff in the vicinity, then with an evil leer pulled a square of crumpled paper from the back pocket of his jeans and thrust it under Jamie's nose, obscuring the maths homework. "Get a load of that, then!"

Jamie glanced at it – but only because he had to; and then as briefly as possible. He said "Yeah", and pushed it to one side.

"Not bad, eh?"

"Not bad," said Jamie. He couldn't think what it was that Doug got out of this everlasting porno of his. Sometimes he wished he'd got the guts to say "Stuff your dirty pictures, they bore me," but of course he hadn't. "Look," he said, irritably, "what the hell is this supposed to mean? If $x^2 = 8,000$ square metres, how in God's name can x end up equalling 8,944?"

"I dunno." Doug was lost in contemplative day-dreams of his piece of porno.

"Well, it can't. Even I can see that." Grumbling, Jamie went back to the beginning and checked through Doug's arithmetic. "Got the flaming point in the wrong place, haven't you?"

"Yeah?" Miss Hargreaves was coming towards them, along one of the gravel paths. Doug stuffed his piece of porno back in his pocket, waited till she'd passed, then rolling over on to his front said: "You and Sharon jacked it in permanently, then?"

He grunted; non-committal.

"She was down the disco with that Pearson creep the other night."

"Oh?" Just as well he hadn't gone there, in that case. Spared himself the aggravation.

"Beats me what they see in him," said Doug. "Apart from the obvious."

He wondered what the obvious was.

"Sure as hell hasn't got anything else going for him."

There was a pause. Jamie copied "$ax^2 + bx + c = 0$".

"Know what I reckon?" said Doug. "I reckon you weren't giving her enough, that's what I reckon."

He grinned, to show that he was joking. But was he joking? Jamie frowned. He copied "$x = -b \pm b^2 - 4ac$" (whatever the hell that meant). Did Doug know that he and Sharon had never – that *he* had never – that the furthest he'd ever got with her was a quick kiss and a cuddle down by the rabbit hutches in her Dad's back yard? It was the furthest he'd ever seriously tried to get with her. He'd always believed that it was the furthest she'd let him get. Maybe he was wrong. Maybe underneath the little goody-goody exterior she was a mass of seething passions, just waiting for some masterful male (B. Pearson?) to enfold her in his powerful embrace and wreak his wicked will.

Viciously, he copied "Either $x = +6 + 7.746 = 13.746 = 2.291$" – the trouble was, he wasn't masterful enough: he wasn't *positive* enough – "Or $x = -6 - 7.746 = -13.746 = -2.291$" (what a load of meaningless twaddle). But then again, how could you be positive when you weren't absolutely certain what it was that you wanted? Or even, come to that, whether you really wanted it? That was the trouble: he couldn't be certain. If only he could, he'd be as positive as anyone.

"Tell you what," said Doug. "We're going down the Folk Club Friday night. I bet if I asked Sandy, she could get Marigold Johnson to come along. How about it?" He winked. "Be all right there. Doesn't give herself airs and graces like old Miss Strait Lace."

No, of course she didn't, thought Jamie. Didn't have anything to give herself airs and graces about, did she? School bicycle, that's what Marigold Johnson was. Practically every boy in the fifth had been out with her at some time or another, except for him. Not that he had anything against her. She was a good sort, was Marigold; he just didn't fancy her, that was all. And anyway, why did people keep trying to push him into going out with people he didn't want to go out with? First it had been Sharon, trying to palm him off with Coral Flashlight; now it was Doug, urging Marigold Johnson on him.

"I can't come Friday," he said. "I'm doing things."

Doug raised his head to look at him.

"Doing things?" How could Jamie be doing things that *he* didn't know about? "What things?"

"Just things," said Jamie.

"What just things?"

"Got to pick my kid sister up from her ballet class."

"Oh! Is that all? Well, that's OK ... come afterwards."

$4^2 - 8n - 1 = 0 -$

"Can't."

"Why not?"

"Can't, 'swhy not."

Normally he could have done, because normally he only picked up Kim and took her back home: his sessions with Anita were in the middle of the week. It was only this particular Friday. They were having what Miss Tucker called "a general run-through", and he had already promised to be there. He felt less than enthusiastic about it (exposing himself in a pair of tights in front of *Kim*?) but at the same time he didn't feel inclined to go letting people down at the last minute only for the sake of an evening spent with Marigold Johnson.

"Come off it!" said Doug. "What d'you mean, you can't, that's why not?"

"If you must know – " $(n = -b \pm b^2 - 4ac)$ – "I said I'd stay on and give a hand."

"Give a hand? With a ballet class?" Doug's voice rose to a screech. "You're giving a hand with a *ballet* class?"

"No, you blithering idiot. I'm giving a hand with a show they're doing."

"Oh!" Doug relaxed. "You had me worried for a moment ... I thought it was a touch of the old monkey fur jock strap and pink hairnet brigade."

"Ha ha," said Jamie.

"Yeah, well, you must admit . . . it would be a bit off. Mind you, with your hair you could almost do with a hairnet. Not surprised old Hubbard had a go at you."

He frowned. There was nothing wrong with his hair; old Hubbard was an ass. He had told him the other day to "go and get that wig lopped before I get a pair of scissors and do the job myself". He had no intention of getting it lopped. He wasn't a skinhead, for God's sake. Anyway, Miss Tucker had said that it was just right. He reckoned she knew a sight more about such things than old Hubbard.

"So what you doing, then?" said Doug. "Electrics?"

"Something like that."

Doug thought about it a while.

"Ballet class, eh?"

Jamie bent his head over his maths book. He hoped they weren't going to harp on it.

"Good place for birds," said Doug.

"Yeah."

"Next best thing to a harem."

"Yeah."

"That what you're doing it for?"

Exasperated, Jamie sat up. He pushed his hair out of his eyes.

"No, it is not, you sex-polluted slob. It happens to be for charity. Some of us round here have minds that rise above the merely animal – and you can take your lousy stinking maths." He slapped the book against Doug's head. "I don't know why I bothered copying it in the first place . . . it's so bloody awful, I could have done better myself."

5

The general run-through on Friday evening hadn't been anywhere near as bad as he'd thought it was going to be. In fact, if he were strictly honest with himself, he would have to admit that he'd got quite a kick out of it. Far from giggling at the sight of him wearing tights, Kim had gone round excitedly telling everyone that "That's my brother"; and all the little girls had stared at him goggle-eyed and accorded him what amounted to almost a sort of reverence. He thought that very probably it was a case of reflected glory, since Anita, quite obviously, was the star of the whole set-up, but nonetheless it made a pleasant change from the open contempt with which the brat-like juniors at Tenterden Road Comprehensive were wont to treat their elders and betters.

On the way home, afterwards, across the Common, with Kim skipping ahead doing her Dewdrop routine, Anita said: "You will be able to come next Sunday, won't you?"

He said "Sunday?" and then "Oh, yeah! Sunday", as if he'd forgotten. He didn't want her getting complacent about it. The only reason he'd agreed to Sunday was because Miss Tucker had asked him specially. "I know you're very busy and probably have things of your own to do, but you needn't stay for the whole rehearsal. Not if you don't want to. It's just that I would have liked to go through your bit with Anita, if at all possible." And then, when she'd thought that he was going to make excuses: "It does mean a great deal to her, you know."

He'd already gathered that for himself. He'd thought Kim had got it badly enough, but Anita was a positive nut case. He'd never yet heard her talk about anything that didn't have some connection with the ballet – he'd noticed that it was always *the* ballet, like it was always *the* opera, which had to be pronounced "oppra" if you were going to be really classy. Anita called it oppra. It was only common people like Jamie who said opperer. Not that Anita seemed to mind. There were some girls in her position who wouldn't have been seen dead with a boy from Tenterden, but to Anita it obviously didn't matter where he came from. So long as he could keep in time to the music and be there on hand when she needed him, that was all that mattered to her. Sometimes he wondered whether she was ever actually aware of him as another human being.

Now, eager, but seemingly just a bit embarrassed as well – which was odd, because he wouldn't have thought her capable of embarrassment – she said: "Are you by any chance doing anything tomorrow?"

What was it with him, that he could never learn the simple lessons of life? Even a cretin would have known to hedge his bets. The correct answer was a cautious "Depends" – and then see what she had to offer. Old Muggins goes and says, "Nothing in particular. Why?"

Well, yes. *Why?* That was the question, wasn't it? Why, for starters, was he such an abject, grovelling buffoon? Did he really expect her to say "Come to a party with me? Come to a disco with me?" Perhaps, poor mutt, he actually did.

"I was wondering," said Anita – and her cheeks, which were usually pale, grew ever so slightly tinged with pink. "I was wondering whether you'd mind awfully putting in a bit of extra rehearsal? The afternoon would be best, but we could make it the morning if you'd rather. It doesn't matter terribly, it's only that I did promise Mummy I'd go up to town with her. We've got this beastly wedding, and she wants to choose outfits, but it's not desperately important. Not nearly as important as being able to rehearse. It's that second lift I'm bothered about. I haven't quite got the timing of it right. I thought – " Her voice faded, uncertainly. He was glad she was uncertain. He felt that she ought to be. "I thought, if you could manage it, that maybe we could do it at my house. There's a proper studio, and everything, and I've got the music. I've got a tape of Marjorie playing it. I did it specially, the other day, just in case." Again, she faltered. "I wasn't sure how you'd feel about it."

He wasn't sure how he felt about it, either. He wouldn't mind seeing inside her house, seeing what it was like, where the rich people lived; on the other hand he didn't want to do anything which would encourage her to start taking his co-operation for granted. This was a favour he was conferring.

"I guess I could come for an hour," he said.

Her face cleared.

"An hour would be perfect! When could you manage it?"

If she was prepared to be humble, then he was prepared to be magnanimous.

"Any time would do me," he said. "Afternoon, if that's what's best."

"About three o'clock? Would that be all right?"

He indicated that it would.

"Oh, that's super!" said Anita.

"So which house do you live in?"

"The one over there – " She pointed, in the direction of the golf course. "The one right at the end, with the green roof. If you're coming over the Common, you'd better use the back entrance, otherwise you'll have to walk for miles. But if you're coming by bus, then you have to get out at Delmey Close and cut up the passage, then walk along. It's all a bit complicated."

"That's OK," he said. "I'll find it."

The house Anita lived in was very new and clean and spacious. He had never seen anywhere so clean and spacious. He was used to the Victorian gloom of the flat above the off-licence, with its long, narrow passages, high-ceilinged but cramped, and its antiquated bathroom with the lead piping all naked and the cast-iron bath which his Mum always swore was going to "come through that ceiling one of these days, sure as eggs is eggs". His Mum had a thing about ceilings. Not surprising, really, since half the floorboards and most of the beams were eaten away with woodworm. A woodworm wouldn't have survived five minutes in Anita's house. It was all metal and plastic and spotless.

He walked there over the Common and went in through the back garden, which was also spotless, with a lawn that looked as if it were rolled up and put away in a cupboard every night to keep it from getting dirty, and all the flowers all bright and polished in their weedless flower beds. He marvelled at it: not an empty Coca Cola tin or cigarette pack in sight. The off-licence didn't have a back garden, only a bit of yard where they unloaded the crates;

but he bet that if it had it would be like a garbage tip, buried fathoms deep under other people's rubbish.

Anita, already changed into her leotard and tights, came running out to meet him through some long french windows which opened on to a paved area full of trailing things in tubs.

"You came!" she said – as if she'd feared perhaps he wouldn't. The thought gratified him. "Come in and get changed. You can use my bedroom, the studio's right next door."

He said: "That's all right. I don't need to change."

She looked at him, doubtfully.

"You're going to stay as you are?"

Yes: he was going to stay as he was, in sweat shirt and jeans. It was his own personal act of assertion.

"You'll get awfully hot," said Anita; but at least she didn't try offering him a pair of tights.

"Where are your parents?" he said, as she led the way indoors.

"Oh, somewhere about . . . I think Daddy's on the golf course. I'm not sure where Mummy is. She might be lying down, she always says going up to town exhausts her."

"Won't it disturb her, then? Us thumping about?"

"We don't *thump*," said Anita. "And anyway, she's right at the other end."

It was only then that he realized: the house was, in fact, a bungalow. He'd never been in a bungalow before. It seemed strange, having everything on one floor. The flat above the off-licence was on two (or two and a half if you counted the bathroom, which had been added on later). He thought that really a bungalow was probably more sensible, except of course that it would take up far more ground space, so that you'd need to be pretty rich if you were going to be able to pay the rates. Great, though, not having to run up and down stairs all the time. His Mum would like that, she wouldn't have to worry herself about the ceilings.

They rehearsed for an hour, in Anita's studio (what Kim wouldn't give, to have a place like that!). They worked as hard as ever Miss Tucker worked them: after only ten minutes, Jamie could feel the perspiration running in rivers down his back. He stuck it for as long as he could, then with a defiant "Hang on a sec" stripped off his sweat shirt and flung it across the room. He dared Anita to say something. He tensed himself, waiting for it. "I told you so, I said you ought to change, I knew you'd get too hot . . ." Sharon couldn't have resisted it. She'd have been right in there, crowing at him. He didn't know whether Anita was more tactful or whether she was so absorbed in what she was doing that she simply didn't notice, but at any rate she made no comment. Only afterwards, when they had worn themselves to a standstill, she gestured towards some pink curtains at the far end of the room and said: "You could have a shower, if you wanted."

There was nothing he would have liked more; but one did, after all, have one's pride. He wasn't admitting he'd made a mistake.

"That's OK," he said.

"Well, if you're sure . . . here!" She flung a towel at him. "You'd better dry yourself."

He wasn't averse to that, since she was doing the same. His hair was so wet it felt as if he'd been in the swimming baths.

"You ought to wear a sweat band," said Anita. "Stop it getting into your eyes."

He looked at her. Innocently, she looked back at

him. She hadn't been criticizing: only trying to be helpful.

"I thought that was pretty good, didn't you? I really thought we made some progess. Don't let's tell Thea about it – let's see if she notices. Then if she does we'll tell her. I know that lift was the one thing she was really worried about. She was wondering whether we ought to do something to simplify it. I told her it would be all right – and now it is! Isn't it?" She regarded him, anxiously. "Don't you feel that it is? Don't you feel happier with it? I do. – You ought to put your jumper back on, by the way. You'll get cold, otherwise. I'll just go and change. I shan't be a minute." She went through into her bedroom, and called out to him through the closed door: "Would you like some tea and biscuits? Or a glass of orange, or something?"

"Wouldn't mind a glass of orange," said Jamie.

Anita reappeared, almost within the promised minute, wearing a plain white dress with a pleated skirt and no sleeves. She looked fresh and cool and smelt faintly of flowers. Jamie, by contrast, felt hot and sticky. His sweat shirt was clammy and clinging to him, and the steam rose up from his jeans as he walked. He thought he probably stank like a thousand armpits. Anita, as usual, seemed not to notice: she was very good at not noticing. He wondered again if she were tactful, or simply self-absorbed. He couldn't quite make her out.

In the huge airy kitchen with its Vent Axia fan (his Mum had always wanted one of those: she was always on about her Vent Axia) they helped themselves to real fruit juice from the refrigerator and took it out with them into the garden. There were still no signs of Mummy and Daddy, for which, in his present state, he was thankful. He could just imagine their joy at seeing *him* out there – probably take one look and order him straight off the premises. Couldn't have nasty common boys like that around, polluting the atmosphere.

Anita walked across the smooth green lawn; gingerly, he followed her. It seemed almost sacrilege to step on the stuff.

"What are those things?" he said, trying to make conversation. He jerked his head at some brightly coloured flowers, nid-nodding in a nearby bed.

"Oh – I don't know," Anita spared them a quick glance. "Mesmeranthus, or something." Plainly, flowers held no interest for her. Perhaps she was too used to them.

"They're pretty," said Jamie.

"Yes. I suppose they are." She studied them a moment, as if seeing them for the first time. "Bracey does all the gardening. He'd know what they were. I could ask him for you, if you like – if you're really interested."

He wasn't as interested as all that. It was just something to talk about. He wasn't sure what one did talk about, with a girl like Anita. She solved the problem for him.

"Tell me," she said. "Did you ever discover whether you *could* do that Russian thing?"

"Russian thing?" he said. He remembered, as he said it, that that was what he'd said last time.

"You know," said Anita. "Like I showed you."

She set down her glass and showed him again, in her plain white dress with the pleated skirt.

"Oh, that," he said.

"*Can* you do it?"

"I should think anyone could," said Jamie.

She tossed her head.

"Garstin can't."

"Oh, well! Garstin."

He had met Garstin last night – a tall, lank youth about the same age as himself. It had been so pathetically obvious, looking at him, that he was the sort of boy who would never be capable of doing anything that required even a modicum of physical strength or co-ordination – the sort of boy who would always, inevitably, be clean bowled first ball and drop every catch that ever came his way – that Jamie had almost felt pity for him rather than scorn. Still, he felt duty bound to say *oh, well, Garstin*: it seemed the accepted response.

"The thing is," said Anita, "that if you *could* do it, we could put the Russian sequence back in the first half. We had to take it out when David broke his arm. There wasn't any use trying to do it with Garstin. But now that we've got you – "

She looked at him, hopefully. He frowned into his orange juice. He didn't care for this "now we've got you" business. They hadn't *got* him. He was there purely as a favour. He could back out right now, if he felt inclined.

"It's tremendously exciting," said Anita. "Thea did the choreography herself. The music's by Borodin – *Polovtsian Dances*. Do you know it?"

"No," said Jamie.

"Oh, I'm sure you do! I'm sure if you heard it – tchum DA dum, tchum DA dum, tchum DA dum – " All of a sudden, she was whirling away across the grass, arms flying, pleated skirt twirling. "Tchum DA dum, tchum DA dum – "

She was quite right, of course: he did know the music. He just hadn't known what it was called. As she danced, he could hear it in his head, all the timpani crashing and banging and the drums going bananas. For a moment he almost felt the urge to join in, but managed just in time to suppress it. This thing had gone far enough; it had to be checked, before it got out of hand.

"Imagine – " Anita, breathless, her eyes bright, came whirling back to him. "Imagine how super you'd look as a Polovtsian warrior! We could give you a moustache – we could make it out of crêped hair – one of those ones that grows right down – " She pencilled it in on his face with the tip of her right index finger. "And you wouldn't have to wear tights! Think of that!"

He thought of it, and said grudgingly: "Why? What would I have to wear, then?"

"Oh, there's a proper Polovtsian warrior get-up! A kind of bolero thing, and a band for your hair, and baggy trousers, and sandals with thongs . . . all fearsomely butch!"

He couldn't see anything fearsomely butch about dressing himself up in a "kind of bolero thing" and sandals with thongs. On the other hand, it was certainly better than tights.

"Oh, do say you'll do it!" said Anita. "Please!"

They had had this scene once before. On that occasion he had allowed himself to be talked round.

"I suppose" – he couldn't help saying it – "I suppose *you* only want to do it because you'll be the star attraction."

She fell back a pace.

"That's a mean thing to say – and it's not even true! If we *don't* do it I'll be the star attraction because then I'll have to fill in with the Sugar Plum Fairy, which I already did last year. And apart from the fact that everyone's probably sick to death with it, it wouldn't fit in nearly so well with the rest of the show. It's the *show* I'm thinking of – that and giving other people a chance. You're more likely to be the star attraction than me. It's a man's thing, not a girl's: I'd only be playing second fiddle. You'd be the one that got all the really exciting things to do."

How could he say, after that, that he didn't want exciting things to do? He found that he was digging divots out of the lawn with the toe of his shoe. With guilty stealth, he began to flatten them back again.

"It seems such a waste," said Anita. "When God's given you a talent for doing something really well – "

He didn't believe in God. At least, he didn't think that he did. But perhaps it would be churlish of him to say so.

" – when there's something you can do that gives positive pleasure to people – "

Yes; jumping around in baggy trousers and a kind of bolero thing. Give them all a big laugh, that would.

"The way I see it," said Anita, "it's like a sort of *duty*."

She made it sound almost holy. Perhaps, to her, it was.

"Yeah. Well – " He placed his foot firmly over the flattened divots. "It's the time factor, you see." Time factor: he liked that. He said it again. "It's the time factor that screws it."

Wilfully, she misunderstood him.

"There's still another four weeks to go, almost. You could easily learn it in four weeks! If we practised like mad – if you came round every Saturday and we really worked at it – "

"What, round here?" he said.

He felt himself weakening. Coming round here was a very different kettle of fish from going to Miss Tucker's. For one thing, he could tell Doug about it.

"I've got this new bird I'm going with. Lives in one of those big houses up by the golf course – "

"Of course," said Anita, in thoughtful tones, "I don't actually know that you can do it yet, do I? I've only got your word for it. For all I know, you could be just as useless as Garstin. I mean" – she looked up at him, demure in her plain white dress – "you haven't actually shown me, have you?"

He had no objections to make: he knew perfectly well that he could do it. He could do it standing on his head.

It was a pity, perhaps, in the circumstances, that he didn't; it would have saved a great deal of embarrassment. As he squatted on his haunches, there was a loud ripping sound. Momentarily, he forgot the company he was in: he gave vent to one of those four-letter words which if his Dad ever caught him at it brought retribution very swiftly in its wake. Anita didn't bat an eyelid. She didn't say "Naughty naughty", or tell him not to use bad language; she only gave him a wicked grin and said: "Just as well that didn't happen when Thea was around . . ."

He couldn't be sure whether she was referring to his jeans parting company, or to him swearing. Either way, it was embarrassing.

6

The following Saturday, at breakfast, Mr Carr said: "You coming down the road with me tomorrow, then?"

"Down the road?" said Jamie. "What for?"

Mr Carr looked hurt.

"One-day match, son!"

"Oh." He'd forgotten all about the one-day match. They always went to them together. Damn! He should have thought of that, before making rash promises. Now what was he going to do?

Before he could say anything, Kim's voice had come shrilling across the table: "He can't tomorrow, we've got a rehearsal!"

"Now, come on, young lady – " Mr Carr wagged a finger at her. "Fair's fair. You can get home under your own steam on a Sunday morning. Don't need your big brother to play escort *all* the time.'

"But he's *in* it!" said Kim.

"In it? In what?"

"In the *rehearsal*," said Kim. "In the *show*."

"What, him?" Mr Carr guffawed, happily. "Doing what? Chasing Dewdrops?"

"Jamie kicked out at Kim beneath the table. He had made her promise that she wouldn't tell anyone. "It's a secret. Understand? Just you and me. You let anyone else into it, and that's that. Finito. Right?"

Kim had said "Right" and solemnly nodded her head. Too late, he realized that he had not specifically included parents in the prohibition. Kim obviously didn't count parents as being "anyone else": they were just parents. She took absolutely no notice whatsoever of his warning kick – probably thought he was just thrashing about for the fun of it.

"Jamie's *dancing*," she said; and then, blissfully: "He's partnering Anita Cairncross."

The way she said it, she made it sound as if Anita Cairncross was the Queen, or Princess Anne, or someone. A minor royal at the very least.

"Is he, indeed? Well, well!" Mr Carr seemed not quite certain how to take this piece of information. "Good old Anita Cairncross! Let's hope she enjoys it. Can't say that I would . . . great clumsy oaf like that."

Kim, who had strictly no sense of humour where her beloved ballet was concerned, said: "Jamie's not clumsy. Miss Tucker says he's the most promising boy she's ever had." Jamie choked on his Weetabix. "She does, Jamie." Kim, all unaware, reached out for a piece of toast and began smearing butter on it inches deep, taking advantage of the fact that Mrs Carr was in the kitchen and couldn't see. "Honest. I heard her talking to Anita. She said, he's the most promising boy I've ever had. And then she said something about, if we could only manage to convince him that it's – and then I couldn't hear any more because they walked away. Could you pass the honey?"

"Please," said Jamie.

"Please," said Kim. She turned, important, to her father. "Jamie and Anita," she said, "are doing a classical pas de deux."

"Oh, yes?" His father was eyeing him, quizzically. "And what's a classical pas de deux when it's at home? Greek father of twins?"

Kim wrinkled her nose, not seeing the joke.

"It's when two people dance together. With lifts, and things."

"Lifts?" said Mr Carr. "You mean the sort that go up and down? First floor, second floor – "

Kim looked at him, scornfully.

"That's in buildings," she said. "Lifts in ballet are something different. It's where the man has to pick the girl up and carry her."

"Oh, is it?" said Mr Carr. "Ah, well, now you're starting to make sense! Picks her up and carries her, does he?"

"Yes, and then he has to support her when she does pirouettes and things." Kim jumped up, over-turning the honey. "Come and show him, Jamie!"

He shook his head, deeply embarrassed. This was worse even than splitting his jeans in front of Anita. Mr Carr, good-humouredly, said: "Never tell me we're going to see those great hairy legs of yours encased in a pair of tights?"

They were back to those blasted tights again. He mumbled, incoherently, into his Weetabix.

"How gruesome!" said Mr Carr. "That'll be a sight for sore eyes, and no mistake."

Kim, sitting herself down again, began scraping honey off the tablecloth.

"Everybody wears tights," she said.

"Yes, but everybody hasn't got great hairy legs, have they?"

"Jamie hasn't got great hairy legs. Miss Tucker says – "

They were spared, thank God, any more of Miss Tucker's utterances by the arrival of his mother bearing bacon and eggs. She had obviously caught most of the conversation, for she said at once: "Who's Anita Cairncross? Is she the girl with the nice voice that rang you up the other day?"

"She's the one he's dancing with," said Kim. "She's the best dancer in the whole of the school. She's going to do it full time next year."

"She sounded really nice," said Mrs Carr. "Not like that other one. That Sharon, or whatever her name was. I never cared for that one. Always thought she'd lead you into bad ways. This one sounded quite different. Where does she live? Near?"

"Over on the Common," said Kim. "By the golf course."

"One of the new houses. Well!" Mrs Carr dished up bacon and eggs. Jamie looked at them unenthusiastically. "Pretty, is she?"

Before Kim could say "She's the prettiest girl in the whole of the school", he said: "Not particularly."

"Jamie, she *is*," said Kim.

"No, she isn't. She's skinny as a rake."

"She isn't skinny, she's slim!"

"Well, whatever she is, she hasn't got any sex appeal."

"A likely tale!" Mr Carr chuckled, as he leaned across to get the teapot. "All I can say is, I wish you the best of British . . . You must have the nerve of Old Nick!"

"*Look*." Jamie slammed down his knife and fork. Everyone, obediently, looked. They seemed startled – he was not one who was much given to wild outbursts. "Look – " He pushed his hair out of his eyes. "It's for charity, isn't it? It's for *spastics*. What am I supposed to say? When they ask me? What do I say? Stuff spastics? Is that what you want me to say? Stuff Auntie Carol and stuff Linda and stuff Fairfield?" He glared at them. "Is it?"

There was a silence. Even Kim was temporarily muted.

"No. Well – " Mr Carr cleared his throat. "Obviously it isn't. We all have to do our bit, the best way we can. Only too glad you've got a social conscience. Better than vandalizing football pitches. So!" Some of his previous joviality returned. "When is it happening, this great event? I take it we shall be allowed to come?"

"You've *got* to come," said Kim. "*Every*body's got to."

"Everybody's got to! Well! That settles it, then, doesn't it?" Mr Carr winked, and ruffled his son's hair – a gesture of paternal affection which Jamie could well have done without. He loathed it when people ruffled his hair. "Don't worry yourself, son! We'll take it seriously."

With any luck, thought Jamie, they wouldn't get the opportunity: with any luck, they'd both of them be struck down with the shingles.

"Doesn't worry me," he said. "It's not my show." He pushed his plate away. "I'm only doing it to help out."

On Tuesday morning, on the way to school, along the path that bordered the woods, he found himself overtaken by Sharon. Surprise, surprise, she stopped to speak.

"Hi, Jamie," she said.

He looked at her, frowningly. "Hi."

She fell into step beside him, moderating her pace to his.

"Be late for school if you don't get a move on."

So, he would be late for school. So it would be the

second time in one week. So what? He had more important things to worry about. She had interrupted him in the middle of going through the steps of the Russian dance, which Miss Tucker had shown him last night. He had been seeing them in his mind, trying to fit them into their proper sequence. If she was so bothered about being late, then let her be the one to get a move on.

It seemed that she was not as bothered as all that. She was obviously disposed to talk and make overtures.

"Did you do that stuff for old Fossil?"

"What stuff?"

"That stuff about Elizabethan poets."

"Oh, that. Yeah." He'd cribbed it out of a book Anita had lent him. Anita went to the High School, which worked a year ahead of everyone else. She'd already done Elizabethan poets.

"I couldn't find anything to say," said Sharon.

"No?" He kicked a stone. He wished she would go away and let him get on with things.

"I just couldn't think of anything – I mean, there *wasn't* anything. I only wrote half a page." She looked at him, hopefully. "How much did you write?"

"Dunno." He shrugged a shoulder. "Couple or so."

"Couple of *pages*?" said Sharon.

"Yeah, well, I write big," he said.

"I know, but *still* – "

For a while there was silence, as she pondered the awesomeness of it. Jamie went back to his Russian dance. He tried to pick it up where he'd left off, halfway through, but it was like saying the alphabet when you were in infant school, unless you started right at the beginning – abcdef*g* – , hijkellemenno*p* – you couldn't get the rhythm of it, you couldn't get the pattern. Blast Sharon. Why did she have to come and talk to him at *this* particular moment? She hadn't been anywhere near him for weeks. Now she'd gone and broken the sequence. He would have to go all the way back and start again.

So. First there were the turning things – yaa-*dum*, yaa-*dum*, yaa-*dum*, yaa –

"Don't seem to see you down the disco these days," said Sharon

"What?" He jerked his head round, irritably. "No. I haven't had the time."

On the morning air came the shrill sound of a bell, marking the beginning of assembly.

"There's the bell," said Sharon.

What did she think, he was deaf, or something?

"I knew we'd be late. If the butcher's open down the bottom of Brafferton, I always know."

Now what was she on about? Butcher down the bottom of Brafferton, for heaven's sake! Exasperated, he broke into a jog.

"Well, don't just stand there, then . . . get a move on!"

In English, when the essays were collected, she turned round and pulled a face at him. It was the sort of face that implied some special kind of relationship: he ignored it. In Civics, a bit later, she patted an empty chair and invited him to sit next to her. Loftily, he pretended not to have noticed and went to sit next to Doug, in the back row, where they passed an agreeable forty minutes seeing how many dirty words they could make out of People's Democratic Republic of Algeria. In spite of all this, she still smiled at him as they went out through the door; and to cap it all, as he sauntered up the road with Doug during the dinner break, they ran into her coming out of the fish shop, and she smiled at him yet again and stuck a chip in his mouth.

"'Oo's a lucky boy?" said Doug.

Next morning, after PE, when they were under the showers, he sidled up to Jamie, and out of the corner of his mouth muttered: "Hey, Buster, you wanna hear sumpun? Woid's on the street that a certain little lady ain't got no gennelman friend no more." And then, reverting to a more normal mode of expression: "I reckon if you were to put in an appearance down the disco Saturday night you'd find she was a pushover."

He toyed with the idea. He was still toying with it when he went round to Anita's on Saturday afternoon. As he stripped off in her bedroom (with her safely shut away on the other side of the door) he tried to imagine how it would be if he were stripping off in Sharon's bedroom (with Sharon very firmly on *this* side of the door). He couldn't make up his mind whether it appealed to him or whether it didn't. *I reckon you'd find she was a pushover* . . . but did he want her to be a pushover?

Well, and why not? He supposed that he ought, if only to show Doug – if only to prove to *himself*. He decided, quite definitely, that he would go. As soon as they had finished he would go straight back home and have a bath, change into something decent and go down to the disco to pick up Sharon. And this time he meant it. This time he really was determined.

He was still determined when they finished rehearsing; but then they went into the garden with their orange juice, and Mummy was out there sunning herself, and Daddy came back from the golf course, and everybody got talking, and he and Daddy talked about cricket, about which Daddy turned out to be quite knowledgeable, and Mummy wanted to know which school he went to, and didn't actually pass out on the spot when he said Tenterden, but instead said musingly: "I've often wondered whether we shouldn't have chosen a comprehensive for Anita"; and then they had the garden to themselves, because Mummy had to go indoors to see about some food, and Daddy had to have a hot bath, to take away the aches and pains after his exertions on the golf course, and just as Jamie was thinking of saying, "Well, I guess I'd better be off, then," Anita said: "Jamie, you *are* going to watch the ballet on television tonight, aren't you?" and before he had a chance to say "What ballet?" or no, he couldn't, he was going out, had hurried on with: "You really *ought* – especially if you've never seen any. *Have* you ever seen any?"

If he'd had any sense he'd have said "Course I have. Loads." (After all, he'd seen the Benton Bluebells, hadn't he?) Instead, like an idiot, he said: "Well, no. Not exactly. But – "

"Oh, but then you must! Jamie, you *must*! It's Fonteyn and Nureyev!"

Too late, he remembered: it was what Kim had been going on about for the past seven days. "Fonteyn and *Nureyev* . . . Fonteyn and NUREYEV", until it had become a sort of ritual, every time she picked up the television paper.

"Honestly," said Anita. "It's not the sort of chance you can afford to miss."

No, and neither was picking up Sharon at the disco. *That* wasn't the sort of chance he could afford to miss.

"The thing is," he said, "I was sort of thinking of going somewhere." What did he mean, *sort* of? He *was* going somewhere. "I was going to go down the disco," he said.

"But Jamie, it's Fonteyn and Nureyev! You can

go down to the disco any time; but Fonteyn and *Nureyev* – surely just for *once* you could stay in?"

Seized with inspiration, he said: "Wouldn't do any good if I did. We've only got the one telly. My old man'd go spare if anyone suggested watching ballet."

It wasn't an absolute and total lie – Mr Carr didn't exactly go spare, but he certainly grumbled quite a lot. On the other hand, not even he would have had the heart to deny Kim the opportunity of goggling at her beloved Nureyev, and if there'd been any really serious friction there was always the old black and white set down in the shop. Still, Anita wasn't to know.

"*I* wouldn't mind," said Jamie. "It's him. All he likes is international soccer and John Wayne shooting up Indians. Then he goes on about how it's him that pays the licence fee so it's him that ought to choose, and – "

"*I* know,' said Anita. "You could come round here."

He stopped, the wind taken out of his sails.

"Round here?"

"Yes! Why not?"

He couldn't bring himself to say: "Because I'm going down to the disco to pick up a bird . . .' He mumbled: "What about your parents?"

"Oh! They won't mind. Why should they? They only ever half watch, in any case. In fact, it would be quite nice," said Anita, "to have someone else who appreciated it, just for once. To have someone else who had a *feeling* for it."

He was flattered, in spite of himself: five minutes later, he was going back home not to have a bath and change into something decent to go down the disco to pick up Sharon, but to have a bath and

74

snatch a quick tea and go back over the Common to watch ballet with Anita.

Why, for goodness' sake, did he always have to be so *feeble*?

7

The ballet was *Romeo and Juliet*, with music by Prokofiev, and according to the *Radio Times* it was going to last most of the evening – a fact which Jamie noted with the same sort of enthusiasm that he noted a period of double maths or physics scheduled for first thing on a Monday morning. He knew he was supposed to be someone who had a feeling, but the only feeling he could dredge up, as gingerly he placed himself beside Anita on a velvet sofa that looked far too fragile for actually sitting on, was the glum anticipation of boredom. If he'd known it was going to go on as long as this, he would never have come; not even to please Anita. And if he'd known it was going to be *Romeo and Juliet* – they'd been subjected to *Romeo and Juliet* last term, with Miss Fosdyke. It was quite the most futile play he'd ever read. Really futile. He hardly imagined that the ballet was likely to be any improvement.

It wasn't, to begin with. Just a load of people pratting about in fancy dress, looking like something out of a Christmas pantomime. Mrs Cairncross, glancing up from a nail-polishing session, said, "Well, it's quite pretty," but one wanted it to be more than just pretty. One wanted there to be some action. All these people in their fancy costumes were all very well, but what were they actually *doing*? Nothing, as far as he could make out. Certainly nothing that anyone else couldn't have done. At least with Benton's Bluebells there had been some real dancing.

He found that he was disappointed, in spite of not having expected very much. He had expected it to be better than *this*. Secretly, he'd been hoping that the old Nureyev guy that everyone raved about would be so impressive that even his Dad, watching back at home, would be forced to sit up and take notice. After all, the fellow must have *some*thing. Kim wasn't the only one to do her bits and pieces over him: even Anita tended to crumble at the edges. A few days ago, she'd been showing him how to do a thing called an entrechat (a complicated sort of leap where you were supposed to beat your heels together in mid-air – no mean feat, as he'd discovered when he tried it). Most people, she'd said, only managed to get as far as a six (pronounced sees). "But as you're so good at jumping I shouldn't think you'd have too much difficulty with a huit (pronounced weet). Not once you've mastered the technique." A trifle jealously, since he hadn't yet mastered it sufficiently to do a trois or even a deux, let alone a six or a huit, he'd said: "What about this Nureyev, then? What can he do?" Her eyes had gone all glassy, sort of glazed over with a mist of reverence, and she'd said: "Oh, well. *Nureyev*." (But not at all in the tones that people said oh-well-Garstin.) "I shouldn't be surprised if *he* could manage a douze . . ."

Whether he could or he couldn't, it didn't seem to Jamie that he was getting much of a chance to show anyone; not in *Romeo and Juliet*. He might be impressing Kim, sitting with her stubby nose glued to the box (he bet she was: he could just picture her) but Kim was so far gone he'd probably only have to scratch his left ear and she'd think he'd performed some kind of miracle. He certainly wasn't impressing anyone else. Mrs Cairncross, blowing on her nail varnish to help it dry quicker, wanted to know whether "that was the one, then . . . the one you've all got crushes on?" And when Anita didn't deign to reply: "When I was your age, it was all film stars. Tony Curtis, I remember." She gave a little laugh. "He was the one I went for." Mr Cairncross only poured himself a large bubble of brandy and said: "Nice pair of legs he's got, I'll say that for him."

It wasn't until the duel scene between Tybalt and Mercutio that things began to liven up. For the first time, Jamie found himself taking notice. This was more like! They were going at it, hammer and tongs, all over the stage. It was one of the best sword fights he'd ever seen. He crouched forward, on the edge of his seat, tense and absorbed, watching every move – not that he didn't know the outcome, because he remembered it perfectly well from last term with Miss Fosdyke. Mercutio had always struck him as being the one decent character in the entire play: he'd been disgusted when Shakespeare had killed him off halfway through. What he was waiting for was the moment when it happened.

When it came, that moment he'd been waiting for, he was like Anita, beside him: eyes riveted, immovable. The death of Mercutio was fantastic. He didn't just lie down and die, he writhed, and rolled, and arched his back – thrashed with his limbs and curled up his muscles and bowled about the stage in hoops of agony. And yet, for all that, it was more than mere acrobatics. Watching Mercutio die he felt almost how he might feel if he were watching someone like, say, Doug. Someone with whom you had had fun, who was always good for a laugh, even if at times you could cheerfully have murdered them.

He wondered which part he would rather dance, if he were to be given the choice: whether he would rather be Mercutio, who at least was a real character, even if he did get nobbled earlier on, or Romeo, who lasted longer but was such a flaming wet, mooning about all the time like some love-sick chicken. He decided he would sacrifice the length and opt for Mercutio. He wouldn't half mind playing that death scene (he made a mental note to try it out in his bedroom sometime when his Mum wasn't around). Of course, he would have to learn how to fence. He wondered how much lessons would cost; whether perhaps it might be a better idea to spend his savings on a fencing foil rather than the guitar he'd promised himself. If he were to buy the fencing foil –

He stiffened, sitting forward again on the edge of his seat. Now it was Romeo's turn. He was having a right go at Tybalt – obviously determined to avenge himself for the death of his friend. That was what Jamie would do, if someone had just killed Doug. He saw himself doing it (he would definitely buy that fencing foil). Maybe Romeo wasn't such a flaming wet after all. He was really putting the boot in there. He'd really got old Tybalt on the run. Any minute now –

"Got him!" Mr Cairncross reached out for his bottle of brandy. Mrs Cairncross, coming back into the room with a tray full of something or other, said: "Which one's that, then?"

"Tybalt," said Anita.

"Tibble?" said Mrs Cairncross.

Anita tightened her lips.

"*Tybalt*," she said.

"Oh! Tybalt. Wasn't he the bullying one? Jamie, have a – "

He wasn't quite sure what it was that she offered him. It sounded like "Have a canopy", but when he took one, not wanting to be thought ungracious, all it was was a bit of toast with a dob of paste smeared on it. It tasted OK, but he was terrified of dropping crumbs and found that in any case you couldn't really concentrate if you were trying to eat at the same time. Perhaps that was why Anita wouldn't have one. He could tell, from the way she frowned and shook her head, without removing her eyes from the screen, that the constant interruptions were irritating her. He bet Kim was suffering in exactly the same way at home. Mr Carr would be there in his armchair, drinking his Guinness and pretending to be watching a football match or a heavyweight title fight, every five minutes taking his nose out of his glass to shout encouragement ("Sock it to him, Rudi baby! Oh, nice one! Nice one!") while Mrs Carr would be clicking with her knitting needles, yanking strands of wool out of crackling plastic bags and looking up at all the crucial moments to ask questions. "What's happening now, then? What's he doing now? Who's been killed?"

Funny how all parents seemed to be alike. He'd have thought Anita's would be different, but obviously they were just as insensitive as everyone else's.

He swallowed his last piece of toast and sat forward, shoulder to shoulder with Anita, his elbows planted on his knees and his hands clamped either side of his head like blinkers, so that he couldn't be distracted. Having despatched the enemy, Romeo had at last come into his own. He'd really got it together now. He wasn't just mooning about any more, he really meant business. You could tell, the way they danced with each other, that he and Juliet had gone further than Jamie and Sharon had ever gone. No snatched kisses by the rabbit hutches in *Juliet*'s back yard: when old Romeo had gone climbing up there to the balcony it had been for more than a good-night cuddle.

He began to revise his opinion of the great Nureyev. Maybe the fellow did have something going for him, after all. Maybe he'd been a bit too hasty, deciding that Mercutio was the part to have. Romeo's sword fight had been just as good as his, and he did still have a death scene to come. He thought that he would wait and see what the death scene was like; see whether it made up for all that mooning about at the beginning.

It certainly wasn't as spectacular as Mercutio's. Romeo didn't do acrobatics and bowl about the stage in hoops. He died quite quietly, by the side of Juliet. In the play, Jamie had thought only what a crass idiot the man was – and had noted with relief that there was only one more page of the rubbish to go. Miss Fosdyke had asked at the end if anyone had found it sad, but no one had; not even any of the girls. When she had applied to Doug to know why not, Doug, in his usual forthright fashion, had said: "Load of cobblers, innit?" And then, when pressed to be more explicit: "Well, I mean . . . her knocking herself out with sleeping pills and him taking poison and her sticking daggers in her chest . . . bloody stupid. Not the way people carry on in real life."

He had spoken for the entire class. They had all voiced their agreement: it *was* bloody stupid: it *wasn't* the way people carried on in real life. Jamie had even added the rider that "Fyou ask me, it ought to be done as a comedy . . . I bet that's what

Shakespeare meant it for, originally. I bet if you did it as a comedy, it'd be one of the funniest things he ever wrote."

Miss Fosdyke had obligingly let them try out the death scene, with Jamie playing Juliet and Doug acting Romeo: all the class had been in stitches. Even when she'd taken them, later, to see a London production with real professional actors, it hadn't been much better. Jamie had still sat stolidly unmoved from start to finish. He didn't know what should make the ballet any different from the play – maybe it was something to do with the music, and not having to listen to all those sloppy words – but whatever it was, when Nureyev as Romeo said goodbye to Juliet for the very last time and lay down by her side to die, he felt a strange burning sensation at the back of his eyes; and when Juliet woke up and found him there, and thought at first that he was just asleep, it really started to get to him. It really did start to get to him. It was like Ave Maria on the organ at his great grand-dad's funeral when he had been the same age as Kim was now. It had done terrible things inside him so that he had wanted to blubber like a kid, even though he'd hardly known his great grand-dad and had actually resented having to go to the funeral in the first place because it meant missing out on a football match. This flaming ballet was doing exactly the same sort of terrible things.

Mrs Cairncross picked up her empty canopy dish.

"I think I'll make some coffee," she said. She walked across to the door, passing in front of the television screen as she did so. "What time, exactly, is this thing supposed to end?"

Mr Cairncross cradled his brandy bubble.

"Any minute now, I should imagine."

"Are you going to give Jamie a lift home?"

"By all means, if he wants one."

Mrs Cairncross paused, one hand on the door knob.

"*Would* you like a lift home, Jamie?"

Hunched forward on the edge of the sofa, seeing the screen through what had now become a definite blur, Jamie pressed so hard with his fingertips against his temples that it actually hurt. He took a breath – through his mouth rather than his nose, because his nose was all blocked up and snuffly – but before he had to risk saying anything, Anita, to his immense relief, had come to his rescue.

"You might at *least* wait until it's finished."

Mrs Cairncross pulled a henpecked face.

"Sorry, I'm sure! I thought it virtually had."

"Well, it virtually *hasn't*. You haven't been watching. How can it be finished when Juliet's still alive?"

Afterwards, when Juliet had killed herself with Romeo's dagger and it really was finished and they were drinking the coffee that Mrs Cairncross had made, they asked him again, "How about this lift, then, Jamie?" but now he was ready for it, and although he still had to breathe through his mouth he was at least able to speak without making a fool of himself. He said, "It's all right, thanks. I don't mind walking," which was quite true, he didn't, but more than that he wanted to be by himself, to go over in his mind what he had just seen, to reconstruct those duel scenes before he had a chance to forget them. He didn't feel like having to make conversation, not even about cars or cricket. He rather thought that Daddy didn't feel like having to bestir himself, either, because when Mrs Cairncross started having doubts about the Common – "At *this* time of night? Jamie, do you think you ought?" – he said bracingly that Jamie was a well set-up lad and that he was quite sure he could take care of himself. "Can't you, young man?" Anita just said: "Honestly, Mummy, don't *fuss* so. There's almost a full moon out there."

In spite of the full moon, as he was passing the wooded area where the nutters flashed and young love went courting, he managed to trip almost headlong over a couple of bodies concealed in the grass. They turned out to be Marigold Johnson and a boy from 5D, whose name he didn't know. The boy from 5D said: "D'you mind watching where you're treading?" Marigold Johnson just looked at him and giggled. He muttered: "Sorry, didn't see you," and walked on, embarrassed. It always embarrassed him when he found people doing things like that. He only hoped to heaven that he hadn't been making mad fencing gestures all by himself. It would be round the school in next to no time: James Carr's going off his rocker. Walks the Common at dead of night making funny motions in the air . . .

He arrived home to find Kim still up, even though it was long past her bedtime. As he climbed the stairs, he heard his mother's voice, exasperated: "Kim, did you hear me? I said, *go to bed*." And Kim's voice, somewhat petulant, in reply: "Yes, all *right*. I'm *going*." There were sounds of feet crossly banging their way over the sitting-room floor, then the door at the head of the stairs was flung open and Kim flounced through, defiant.

"*Anyway*," she said – it was obviously intended as a parting shot – "football's only a *game*. Ballet dancers have to work *far* harder than *foot*ballers."

"Get away with you!" That was his Dad, all masculine and jovial. "Knees bend and point your toes ... call that work? Load of old nannies! Wouldn't last five minutes."

Kim turned red – she looked almost as though she might be going to burst. Jamie knew that she was wrestling with the urge to say something rude, such as "Pig's *bum*", which was the worst thing she was acquainted with just at this moment. He sympathized with her, but hoped for her sake that she managed to suppress it. After a struggle that lasted several seconds, she said: "You put one of your rotten footballers in one of Miss Tucker's classes and *he* wouldn't even last *one* minute."

"You're dead right he wouldn't!" Mr Carr chuckled. "Be too busy running for his life."

Kim opened her mouth to retort, but her mother got in first: there was a note of warning in her voice.

"If I have to tell you again – "

"Oh, all *right*," said Kim. "I'm going."

Huffily, she left the room, elbowing her way past Jamie as if he wasn't even there. They heard her stumping up the stairs and along the passage overhead.

"You shouldn't tease her like that," said Mrs Carr. "It's not fair."

"Go on!" Mr Carr grinned, unrepentant. "Load of old nannies, the lot of 'em." He winked at Jamie across the room. "Where've you been, then? Out on the razzle?"

"Been out with Doug," said Jamie. He didn't quite know why he said it, except that he wasn't in a mood for having his leg pulled, and if he said "round at Anita's" his Dad would never be able to resist the temptation. "Went down the disco. Down Bell Street."

He only hoped Doug wouldn't ask him, Monday morning, why he *hadn't* been down the disco, down

Bell Street. He had a sneaking sort of feeling, which he tried hard to suppress, that it was where he ought to have been. *Romeo and Juliet* with Anita was all very well, but it wasn't actually proving anything, was it? Chickening out at the last minute, that was how some people would have seen it. After all, Sharon was going to have been a pushover, wasn't she? Sharon was going to have been his for the asking. And he'd gone and chosen *Romeo and Juliet*, instead. Deliberately missed out on his chance. Turned his back on the sort of opportunity that might never come his way again, because by this time next week she'd probably have found herself someone else and be back to giving him the cold shoulder once more. She wasn't the sort of girl to hang about; not Sharon.

He decided, as he followed Kim up to bed, that first thing Monday he would ask her, "Doing anything next Saturday?" And if she said no, or even if she just made faint noises, then he would go ahead and make a date. A *firm* date. This time he meant it. This time he *really* meant it.

8

He had hoped, next Monday, that he might bump into Sharon again on his way to school, but of course he didn't: no one was ever around when you wanted them to be. Instead, scuffing his way up the lane through the usual weekend debris, he found a page of porno. It was blowing about in the breeze, amongst all the rest of the rubbish, and it wrapped itself round his legs so that he had to bend down and peel it off.

Normally he would have given it a mere cursory glance and left it where it was: today, in his new role of Casanova-Don Juan, he picked it up to have a closer look. If it did things to Doug, then it ought to do things to him. Obviously naked ladies were what turned everyone else on (he'd even caught his Dad snatching a crafty glance at page 3 of the *Sun* when his Mum wasn't around) so maybe it was just a question of acquiring the taste, like with beer and whisky. The first time he'd swallowed half a pint of beer he'd thought he was going to bring up. He almost quite liked it now. Whisky still defeated him, but then whisky still defeated Doug, so he didn't feel too badly about it. It was this other thing that really bugged him. It was that he'd got to do something about. He guessed he might just as well start now, with a page of naked ladies.

To his unutterable astonishment, the naked ladies turned out not to be naked ladies after all, but naked men. He stared, unbelievingly. Doug had never shown him anything like that. To think that they actually *printed* that sort of thing – that real people actually *posed* for it. That other real people actually went into shops and *bought* it. He'd thought naked ladies were bad enough; but this –

"What's that you've got there, son? Something interesting?"

Jamie spun round, his face a crimson sunset. A copper was standing there. He must have crept up on him quietly, on purpose.

"Nothing," said Jamie. He crumpled his hand, defensively, over the paper.

"Nothing, eh?" The copper advanced a step towards him. He was one of the young ones: they were always the worst. "Won't mind if I take a look at it, then, will you?"

One ought to be able to say yes – one ought to be able to tell him to go and get stuffed, that it wasn't any of his business. Doug had tried that once, when they'd wanted to look in his bag and see if he was carrying stolen property (which he wasn't). He'd ended up down at the station being threatened with prosecution for obstructing the law.

"Come on, sunshine! Hand it over."

Jamie did so.

"I found it," he said.

"Oh, yes?" The copper took a look. His face grew a sort of mottled colour. Sort of dark purple with blotches. "You dirty little bastard!" He said it contemptuously, almost viciously. "You filthy dirty little bastard!"

"Look, I *found* it," said Jamie.

"What difference does that make? You didn't have to stand there gawping at it, did you?"

"I wasn't gawping at it. I just picked it up. I didn't know what it was."

"Didn't know what it was! Don't give me that. I saw you, feasting your eyes. Ought to be ashamed of yourself. Kid your age. Can't you think of anything more healthy to do? Have to stand about gorging yourself on obscenities? I tell you, sunshine, if I ever catch you at it again – " He pulled a notebook out of his pocket. "What's your name?"

Name? He was going to take his *name*? Just for picking up a bit of porno off the ground? Jamie swallowed. He'd heard about the police throwing their weight around. It had happened to Doug, it had happened to others. There was a black kid in his class had been hauled up on a breaking and entering charge when he hadn't been anywhere near the place and had half a dozen witnesses to prove it. Jamie had always sworn that if they tried it on with him he'd stand up for himself, he'd know what his rights were. Now it was happening and he found that he didn't; and even if he had he'd have been too scared to do anything about it. He was paralysed with the fear that his parents would be told – that his Head Master would be told – that he himself would be paraded before the whole school: the boy who gorged himself on obscenities.

"Well, come on, lad, I haven't got all day!"

If he had any nous, he'd give a false name. Christopher Marlowe, or John Milton, or something. That's what Doug would have done. He'd told them once he was Perkin Warbeck, and they'd actually believed him. Obviously, Doug had nous. Equally obviously, Jamie hadn't.

"James Carr," he said.

"C-A-double-R?" said the copper.

It wouldn't have done any good, anyway. He knew which school he went to. They'd simply hold an identity parade.

"All right then, James Carr." The copper closed his notebook with a snap. "You have been warned. In future, you keep your perverted tendencies to yourself. There's decent kids use this footpath. I'm not having them corrupted by the likes of you. Now you can hoppit. Go on!" He jerked his head. "Scoot!"

He scooted. He couldn't scoot fast enough. He realized, later, that the copper must have been a nut case. He wouldn't be at all surprised if the bloke weren't a bit kinky, getting all steamed up like that. They oughtn't to have coppers that were kinky. Not if it meant going round accusing people of things they weren't guilty of. Telling him to keep his perverted tendencies to himself – he hadn't *got* any perverted tendencies. He'd picked up what he'd thought were going to be naked ladies and they'd turned out to be naked men. It was a mistake that anyone could have made. Even Doug could have made it. Let them try accusing *him* of perverted tendencies. He'd have them up for slander.

By way of solace, when he approached Sharon during the mid-morning break and asked her whether she was going down the disco Saturday night, she was quite civil to him. Indeed, she was more than civil: she was positively effusive.

"Oh, Jamie," she said, "I wish I could. But I can't. Not Saturday." She sounded genuinely regretful. "We've got to visit these relations. I could make it Friday. Friday I'm not doing anything."

Friday. He was supposed to be rehearsing on Friday. The show was going on in two weeks, and

Miss Tucker was starting to grow anxious. Well, and so was he. *And* with more cause.

"OK," he said. "Let's make it Friday."

"Go down the Folk Club?"

"If that's what you want."

"Don't you like it there?"

"Yeah. I like it." He was prepared, in the present state of truce, to like anywhere she chose to name. The Folk Club, besides, had the advantage that it meant walking back across the Common; and the Common late on a summer's night was notorious. You could hardly move for bodies in the grass.

"What about your sister?" said Sharon. "Don't you have to pick her up?"

"She'll have to take the bus," he said. "It won't hurt her for once."

He left it till the very last minute before he said anything. He ought to have told Miss Tucker, when he went along as usual on Wednesday, but she was all busy and bothered because one of the Dewdrops had gone down with the chicken pox and another had reported "not feeling well". At the end, as he was nerving himself, she put an arm about his shoulders and said: "Good boy! That was excellent. We'll just give that ending a bit of a polish on Friday and it'll be fine." That needn't, of course, have stopped him telling Anita as they walked home together afterwards. There really wasn't any excuse for not telling Anita. It was just that he couldn't stand the way she'd look at him, with her green eyes all reproachful, as if he were proposing to commit some heinous crime such as treason.

On Friday evening at tea he said to Kim: "By the way, you'll have to get the bus back tonight. I won't be able to come and pick you up."

Kim's eyes, round and brown in her little chubby face, were not so much reproachful as outraged.

"But it's a *rehearsal*," she said.

"I know it is. I can't make it."

"Why can't you?"

"Because I can't." Why did everybody always have to question him? "I've got something on at school."

"You can't miss a rehearsal just for something on at school!" Kim's voice was shrill with accusation. "You've *got* to come. You *said* you would."

"I didn't say I would." Everyone had simply assumed that he would. They seemed to forget that he was doing them favours. "You'll have to tell Miss Tucker for me. Tell her it was something I couldn't get out of." After all, whichever way you looked at it, school was a damn sight more important than some pisspot little ballet show. "Tell her I'm sorry, but it came up at the last moment."

"Why? What is it?" said Kim.

He wondered if she was really suspicious, or if it were just his guilty conscience at work.

"Something to do with exams. 'O' levels."

"*All night?*" said Kim.

"Someone's coming to talk to us. It'll probably go on for an hour or two. Then there'll be questions." It was amazing how glibly you could lie once you got started. He even found himself halfway to believing it. Growing cross, he said: "Anyhow, never you mind. Just you make sure that you tell her, that's all."

The Folk Club was hellish; nothing but a succession of nurdling idiots strumming on guitars and droning your actual authentic folk songs. With a hey nonny ho nonny, fol diddle di do, whey hey my lassie-oh. They all sounded exactly the same, and were all sung by middle-aged trendies with bushy beards and high-pitched voices which tended to wander off key and crack at all the crucial moments. There was positively nothing to relieve the tedium save thoughts of what was to come after, when they walked back home across the Common. He had had a bath in preparation, and dressed all in clean clothes and borrowed some of his Dad's aftershave. He felt ready for anything. He felt that tonight he really *could*. He would be firm and masterful, and not take no for an answer. According to Doug, that was how you had to treat girls like Sharon.

"Push 'em about a bit. Show 'em you mean business."

He was hoping that she wouldn't need any pushing about. He had these rose-coloured visions of her gazing up at him out of eyes gone all liquid, clasping both arms about his neck and whispering sweet nothings in his ear. He knew it wouldn't really happen that way. For one thing, eyes that were bright and beady like a sparrow's couldn't possibly go liquid; and for another, he couldn't imagine her Ladyship under any circumstances whispering sweet nothings. Not to him. Still, he hoped that she would at least co-operate. It would be difficult to be masterful if she simply turned on her heel and walked away. But if Doug were right, there wasn't much danger. If Doug were right, she was screaming for it.

Certainly she had no objections to make when he suggested that maybe they'd had enough of the nurdling idiots for one night and ought to go off and get a meal somewhere. She agreed instantly, without even a show of hesitation; though whether it was the prospect of food which enticed her, or whether it was the prospect of walking home across the Common – or whether, perhaps, she was simply as bored as he was with all the hey nonny no-ing – he had not the least idea. Sharon wasn't a girl for giving things away: she liked to keep you guessing.

He stood her a milk shake and a king-size burger and chips in a new hamburger bar that had just opened up. It cost the earth, and meant that he was going to have to plunder his fencing foil fund, but for once he didn't begrudge it. Normally, with Sharon, he would have done, because everyone knew she received astronomical sums of pocket money. Her Mum went out to work specially in order to provide her with it, and when she'd got it she spent it all on herself, on clothes. She had the most extensive wardrobe of any girl in the school. This evening she was wearing a bright pink top with some sort of sparkly stuff sewn round the neck and a black satiny skirt with a slit down the side. He guessed she looked pretty good in it. It wasn't the sort of gear which Anita would have worn, but then Anita was different. He supposed it had to be said that she was superior. At any rate, she was well out of his league.

After the hamburgers, they walked back across the Common. It was neither quite dark nor quite light, but somewhere dusky in between. He wondered if Sharon found it romantic. Experimentally he slipped an arm about her waist: she let it remain there, making no attempt to pull away. Emboldened, he tightened his embrace.

"Know what?" said Sharon.

"No," said Jamie. "What?"

"I reckon I could've sung better than that lot."

"I reckon you could," said Jamie.

They reached the chalk pits, where a couple of young kids, they couldn't have been more than

eleven or twelve, were messing about on motor-
cycles that didn't have either lights or licence plates.
He and Doug had tried that once, on Doug's
brother's bike, but it was a mug's game. There was
always some busybody walking his dog or his bird
who took exception and threatened to have the law
on you.

"Honestly," said Sharon. She sounded aggrieved.
"They oughtn't to be doing that. They might kill
someone."

"More likely kill themselves," said Jamie, remembering the number of times he and Doug had ended
up, minus bike, at the bottom of the pit. It had been
a miracle they'd never broken anything.

"You ought to stop them," said Sharon. "You ought
to say something."

"Like what?"

"Like tell them you'll report them, or something."

He was revolted.

"I'm not a flaming informer!"

"It's for their own good," said Sharon. "They
oughtn't to be doing it."

"Oh, let them alone!" He swung her in the other
direction. "They're enjoying themselves."

"But they oughtn't to be *doing* it."

So what? Had she never done anything she
oughtn't? He wondered how it was that she had this
knack of always managing to irritate.

"Shall we go into the woods?" he said.

"What for?"

"Be nice in there. Nice and quiet."

"It'd be dark," said Sharon. "You couldn't see
where you were going."

"So who wants to?"

Sharon, apparently. She refused point blank to go
into the woods. She said she'd rather walk up to the

look-out and see all the lights marking the roads that led to London.

"Sometimes you can see St Paul's, Mr Hubbard says. If the conditions are right."

He didn't believe that; St Paul's must be all of forty miles away. Most likely what the Hubbard had said was that you could see as *far* as St Paul's. Still, he wasn't going to argue with her; it wasn't worth it.

Duly they trudged as far as the look-out: duly they gazed upon the lights. At least they were alone up there. Perhaps it was quite a good place to have come. The hillside sloped away before them, invitingly covered in ferns and long grass. He wondered how one began.

"Want to come and sit down?" he said.

"Not particularly." She was still searching in vain for St Paul's. "He said the sky had to be clear. I expect there's too much cloud."

"Yeah, I expect so." Anything to keep her happy. He caught her about the waist. "Come and sit down."

She wrinkled her nose.

"On the ground?"

"Why not?" What did she expect? A room at the Ritz? "It's perfectly OK. It hasn't rained for decades."

"It rained last Sunday," said Sharon.

"Yeah, well, that was days ago. It's had a chance to dry out since then. See?" He bent down and rubbed his hand over the grass to show her. "Dry as a bone."

"Yes," she said, "but it might be dirty."

Jesus! Some people. He peeled off his sweater.

"There! How about that?"

Yes: she liked that. Had a touch of the old Walter Raleigh about it. Graciously, she sat herself upon it. He sat down beside her.

"Of course, there isn't any moon," said Sharon. "That would probably make a difference."

Oh, bound to, bound to. (How was one supposed to stop them *talking*, for goodness' sake?)

He slipped his arm back round her waist, and obligingly she wriggled closer. This was better, thought Jamie. He was obviously getting the hang of it. It was simply a question of being masterful.

He tried kissing her, and instead of presenting herself with lips all puckered and pursed like a prune she actually parted them slightly, as if to indicate willingness. He began to feel that Doug had, quite definitely, been right: this was what she had wanted all along. All it had needed was a bit of positivity.

Encouraged, he slid his hand inside her bright pink top with the sparkly things round the neck. Instantly, she pulled away.

"Ja-*mie*!"

"What's the matter?"

"*Don't*."

She only said it because she thought she had to; because it would have looked bad if she'd just let him go ahead without making any form of protest. She was just playing hard to get, that was all. "Push 'em about a bit – show 'em you mean business." What she needed was someone to be masterful. Very well, then.

"*Do you mind?*" Something went stinging like a whiplash across his face: it took him a second to realize that it was Sharon, belting him one. "You just keep your hands to yourself! I didn't come up here to be mauled about."

He might have retorted, then what did you come for? (bearing in mind that the Common was notorious) but he was still reeling from the blow she had dealt him. He wouldn't be at all surprised if she'd broken his nose. For such a puny creature, she packed one hell of a powerful punch.

"You must be bonkers!" Already she was up on her feet, trampling with cold disregard all over his sweater. "You must be out of your tiny mind!"

Jamie thrust a lock of hair out of his eyes.

"There's no need to get all uptight."

"You've got a nerve!" shrieked Sharon. "You bring me up here and maul me about and then tell me that *there's no need to get all uptight?*"

"Well – be reasonable." He wondered if he had red marks across his face, and if so whether they'd be gone by Monday. "There are some girls that actually like it."

"If you think," said Sharon, "that I'm one of *that* sort, then you obviously don't know very much about girls, that's all I can say."

They walked back home with half a yard of daylight between them. All his attempts at apology met with a cold rebuff; she kept saying, "If you thought I was *that* sort of a girl – " When he protested that he hadn't thought she was that sort of a girl (which was perfectly correct, he never had, it was Doug who'd told him she was screaming for it) she only looked at him frostily and said if he didn't think she was that sort of a girl then why had he done what he did?

"Done what?" said Jamie. "What did I do?"

"You know," said Sharon, with heavy emphasis.

"Well, all right, then, so I'm sorry. I made a mistake."

"Yes: you thought I *was* that sort."

You just couldn't win. He gave up trying, after that: they walked the rest of the way in stony silence.

He wondered glumly, as he deposited Sharon at her front gate (she unbent sufficiently to say "If you promise on your *honour* to behave yourself, then I might manage to be free next Saturday," but he wasn't interested any more) where he had gone wrong. Doug knew what he was talking about where girls were concerned. He might not be any great shakes at anything else, but he did know about girls. If he said Sharon was a mass of seething passions, then a mass of seething passions she was, even if she hadn't yet woken up to the fact herself. Obviously what she needed was someone like Doug to come along and rouse her. Jamie, far from rousing her, had only repelled. Probably there wasn't another boy in the whole of Tenterden who could have botched it like he had.

He arrived back home to find the shop already closed for the night and his parents watching television. He stuck his head round the door and said "I'm going upstairs" and disappeared again before his mother could start asking questions, like "What did the man talk about?" and "Don't you want any supper?" He didn't feel like telling any more lies, and he didn't feel like supper. He just wanted to go to bed; to creep into the privacy of his own sheets and brood.

He was in the process of doing so when there was a perfunctory tap at the door and Kim came bursting in. He swore at her – partly because he was half naked and partly because how many times had he told her, "You wait to be asked before you come into my room. Right?" Kim took no notice of his swearing. With an air of self-righteousness, she said: "I told Miss Tucker about you not coming. She wasn't very happy."

He grunted. He didn't want to know about Miss Tucker not being very happy.

"*And* I had to wait nearly forty minutes for the bus," added Kim.

"Good." Jamie took a flying leap into the middle of his bed and pulled the sheet up to his chin.

"I don't see why you say it's good." Kim was obviously in an aggressive mood and spoiling for a fight. "I don't see what's good about someone having to wait forty minutes for a bus."

"Shove off," said Jamie.

"No! Why should I? I had to wait *forty minutes*. And then when it came – "

"Look, I said shove off," said Jamie. "Go on . . . beat it!"

Kim beat it: but not without defiantly putting her head back round the door to say: "Anyway, Anita sent a message for you. She wants to know whether you can make it by two o'clock tomorrow. Round her place."

"No," said Jamie, "I flaming well can't!"

He was sick to death of the lot of them – and that included Anita. He must have been mad, ever getting himself mixed up in all this in the first place. He had a damn good mind to call a halt right now.

"You're to let her know," said Kim. "I said you'd phone her when you got in. That's now," she informed him, in case he was too thick to have realized.

He picked up his pillow and hurled it at her. His mother ought never to have had that brat. She was nothing but a pain.

9

As always, he found himself pathetically unable, at the moment of truth, to say no: punctually at two o'clock the next day he was round at Anita's.

"Thank goodness you could come!" she said. "Last night was an absolute shambles – poor Thea was practically tearing her hair. Karin's chicken pox was only an allergy, but Zoë's gone and got mumps and that wretched child Andrea turned up without her shoes and had to go all the way home for them, and what with one thing and another it was just absolutely *ghastly*. I said that you and I would get on and practise by ourselves, so that Thea could concentrate on the rest of them." She hustled him indoors, as if there wasn't a minute to lose. "The parents have gone out, they won't be back till six-thirty, so we can go on for just as long as it takes."

"Oh, no, we can't," he said. He said it purely as a matter of principle. When would these people ever learn? *He* was the one who was doing the favours. "I can't stay any later than six, I've got to get back."

"Oh! Well – six is all right. Just so long as we *work*. I want to get it really perfect – really spot on. So that when we show Thea tomorrow – "

"Tomorrow?" he said. "What's with tomorrow?"

"There's a rehearsal, in the morning. At the

Church Hall. Oh, Jamie, don't say you can't make it! Not again!"

He was nettled. What did she mean, not again? He was the one that should be saying "not again". It was the second Sunday running.

"I don't know that I can," he said.

"But it's tomorrow morning! If you don't know *now –* "

"I might have something else on, mightn't I?" he said. "I might have made other plans, mightn't I?"

Anita looked at him.

"*Have* you?" she said.

"No, I haven't! I just like to be asked, that's all."

Her face cleared.

"Well, then, I'm asking . . . please, Jamie, will you come?"

He wasn't prepared to be that easily won round.

"What time is it?"

"Nine o'clock till two-thirty."

"Nine o'*clock*?" He wasn't usually out of bed by nine o'clock on a Sunday.

Anita, anxious to mollify, said: "I expect it wouldn't matter if you were a tiny bit late. You probably wouldn't be wanted right away."

Jamie grunted. He knew he was being churlish, but that was the way he felt.

"Truly," said Anita, "we didn't mean to take you for granted. We would have asked you yesterday, only you weren't there."

"I had something on yesterday."

"Yes, I know. Kim told us. Oh, Jamie . . . *please*."

Perhaps he had a power complex, he thought. Perhaps what he secretly wanted was for people to grovel.

"If you don't turn up I simply don't know what we'll – "

"Yeah, OK! OK!" Suddenly, he was bored by it. Mostly what he was bored by was his own pretence that he had it in him to say a firm *no* and to mean it. "Don't keep on," he said. "You've made the point."

In spite of feeling churlish, he didn't set out on purpose to louse things up. He tried his best – his heart just wasn't in it. As a rule, when once he'd got started, he was able to forget all his secret misgivings. So what if his old man did pull his leg? His old man was just a philistine anyway. As for Doug – well, Doug wasn't here, was he? Doug need never know. And even if he did, so what? What was so peculiar about people dancing? When you actually stopped to think about it? Where was the difference between dancing and running, or dancing and swimming, or even, if it came to that, dancing and playing football? They were all physical, weren't they? They all represented a challenge. The way he saw it, if some people could run a mile in under four minutes, then so could he; likewise, if Rudolph Nureyev could do an entrechat douze (*if* he could) then he would jolly well learn to do the same.

Today, he couldn't have cared less about Rudolph Nureyev and his entrechat douze. They were very far from the forefront of his mind. He was still brooding on last night, and the way that he had messed it up with Sharon. Even now he didn't know where he was supposed to have gone wrong. When he was masterful, she slapped his face: when he wasn't, she rejected him for louts like Bob Pearson. Even Doug said that Bob Pearson hadn't got anything going for him – "except the obvious". He never had explained what the obvious was; but whatever it was, it seemed pretty clear that Jamie hadn't got it. Doug had – Bob Pearson had –

"Jamie, what are you *doing*?" said Anita. "That's

the *second* time." She jabbed the stop button on the cassette player and regarded him with an air of exasperation. "What on earth is the matter with you?"

A good question, he thought. A very good question.

"*Well?*" Anita put her hands on her hips.

"Well – " He didn't say "well what?" There didn't seem much point.

"I thought we were supposed to be rehearsing?"

"So that's what we're doing, isn't it?"

"No, it is not!" She stamped a foot. "What we're doing is just wasting time. I don't know why you bothered coming in the first place, if this is all the effort you're going to make."

"Neither do I," he retorted, "if this is all the thanks I'm going to get."

"Well, but Jamie, *honestly*. You might just as well not be here."

He scowled.

"I'm almost beginning to wish that I wasn't."

"Why? Just because you're not concentrating and I'm getting mad at you? I think that's rotten! I think that's really rotten! You wouldn't behave like it if Thea were here."

No, he wouldn't. That was quite true. He felt a pang of conscience.

"The thing is – " He kicked with his toe against the wall. "The thing is, I don't reckon I ought to be doing this lot."

She stared at him.

"Why not?"

He hunched a shoulder.

"Why not?" said Anita.

"I dunno. Just doesn't seem – right, I s'pose."

"What do you mean, it doesn't seem right?"

Questions, questions. Always questions. He shook his head.

"Warriors dance," said Anita. "Look at Red Indians – look at African tribes. It's always the men."

Jamie said nothing.

"What about Zulus?" said Anita. "What about Cossacks? What about the Red *Army*?"

There was a silence. Perhaps if one were a Zulu, thought Jamie, it might be different. But one wasn't. One was a pupil at Tenterden Road Comprehensive, and if word of this ever got out one would be a laughing stock.

"I just don't see what the problem is," said Anita.

No, of course she didn't. She was a girl – it was all right for girls. If *they* were good at dancing, everyone said "how nice". If, on the other hand, they wanted to do metalwork or play football, nobody turned round and said it wasn't right or it wasn't natural or there must be something wrong with them. Not these days. They wouldn't dare. Find themselves up before the Equal Opportunities thingummy before they knew where they were. They could scream till they were blue in the face about their flaming women's lib, he still reckoned they had it a damn sight easier.

Anita was looking at him; awaiting an explanation.

"My Dad" – he cringed, even as he heard himself say it – "my Dad says dancers are a load of old nannies."

"Oh, well! Your Dad!" Anita tossed her head, disdainfully. "It's the stupid sort of thing someone's dad would say, isn't it?"

He supposed that it was. All the same, it didn't alter the fact: messing about in tights and ballet

105

shoes wasn't natural. Not for a boy from Tenterden Road Comprehensive.

"I bet *your Dad*," said Anita, "doesn't know the first thing about it . . . I bet he couldn't even tell an entrechat from an arabesque."

Dead right he couldn't. Probably never even heard of them. He wished, though, that she wouldn't say "your Dad" like that. It sounded wrong, coming from her lips; patronizing, almost. He knew very well that she didn't call her own father "Dad".

"Anyway," said Anita, "you surely don't take any notice of what people *say*? Especially when it's not true. I mean, I know *Garstin*'s a bit of an old woman, but you can't judge everyone by him. In any case, Garstin's not a dancer. David was, and *he's* not – an old woman, I mean. I think he might be gay, but that's something else. No one could say he was *wet*. As a matter of fact, he's a bit like you."

He wondered, rather sourly, whether he was supposed to be comforted by this piece of information.

"It's all so *silly*," said Anita. "What on earth does it matter?"

He felt like saying, "If you went to Tenterden Road Comprehensive you'd *know* what it mattered," but the moment passed and he didn't. He didn't say anything; just frowned and tried to push his hair out of his eyes, only it wasn't in them because he'd taken Anita's advice and worn a sweat band. Anita sighed.

"Thea said we'd have trouble. She said you'd think it was compromising your masculinity."

For crying out loud! What did they *talk* about, those two?

"I don't think it's – " Irritably, he cleared a frog from his throat. "I don't think it's *compromising my masculinity*."

106

"All right, then! So why don't you want to do it? If you're not scared that it's soppy and that people are going to laugh at you, why don't you want to do it? Because you *are* scared that it's soppy and that people are going to laugh at you! You are, and you just won't admit it! You're such a *coward*."

"No, I'm not."

"Yes, you are! It bothers you, what other *people* might think. *You* don't think it's soppy, but – "

"How do you know?" he said. "How do you know I don't?"

"Because if you did you wouldn't be any good at it – you couldn't be any good at it. And you *are* good at it. And anyway, you didn't think *Romeo and Juliet* was soppy, did you?"

He grunted, non-committally.

"*Did* you?" said Anita.

"It was all right. Bits of it."

"Which bits?"

"Bits with the swords; they were OK. But they weren't ballet."

"Yes, they were!"

"No, they weren't."

"They were done by dancers – "

"Yes, but they weren't *ballet*." He lunged, with an imaginary sword. "They were fencing." Feint – parry; cut – thrust. He'd got the whole of one sequence almost completely worked out by now. He'd been practising it in secret, in his bedroom. "I wouldn't mind doing *fencing*." Attack – two, three. Lunge – two, three. "I'm thinking of saving up to buy a foil and have lessons."

Anita stood watching a moment, then: "I've got a fencing foil," she said.

He stopped.

"Where d'you get one?"

"Had it for school. They said we could choose . . . either cricket or fencing. So I did fencing."

His heart swelled. Some people, he thought, bitterly. Some people just had all the luck, didn't they?

"Hang on," said Anita. "I'll get it."

She disappeared into her bedroom. He heard a cupboard door open, heard her rummaging about amongst what sounded to be a collection of tennis rackets and hockey sticks. It probably wouldn't be a real fencing foil; not the sort that real fencers used. Probably just some tinpot, half-size job fit for schoolgirls to mess about with.

"Here it is." Anita had come back. She held something out to him: a real, bona fide, full-size fencing foil, with a button on the end of the blade and a proper metal guard between the blade and the handle. His heart swelled almost to bursting. Some people had *all* the luck. "You can have it," said Anita, "if you like."

He gaped at her, speechless.

"I won't be wanting it any more. I'm going to ballet school next term."

"But – " He gulped. "What about the rest of this term?"

"Oh, I'll tell them I've lost it. I can always use one of the school ones. It really doesn't matter, you don't *have* to have your own. I've only got one because of this friend of Daddy's who used to be a professional. He gave it to me for my birthday."

He was still uneasy – torn between the burning desire to possess, and the feeling that a fencing foil was not something to be given away lightly. Not, at any rate, without parental permission.

"Won't this friend of Daddy's object?"

"Don't suppose he'll ever know. Anyway, I *want* you to have it – I'd *like* you to have it. You ought to

108

have a helmet and a jacket as well, really, but if you're going to take lessons they're bound to provide you with them."

He grew excited.

"D'you reckon?"

"They'd have to. It's dangerous without. You could get stabbed in the eye, or almost anything. Shall I show you how to hold it?" She took the blade away from him, turning it over so that it seemed to him it was the wrong way up, but Anita said no, that was how you had to do it. "Right in the palm of your hand, with your thumb placed flat . . . then you can either bend your wrist *this* way – or *that* way, depending what movement you're doing . . . see? It's quite easy, once you're used to it. Shall I show you the on-guard position? Like this. Look – " She demonstrated, feet apart, at right angles, knees bent, sword arm extended, left arm raised, left hand gracefully curved. It looked almost like a ballet position. "Shall I show you how to attack? I'll show you how to lunge – "

She showed him how to lunge, and how to parry, and how to riposte – she showed him the basic positions – prime and seconde, and tierce and quinte, and several others which he promptly forgot – she showed him how to engage, and how to disengage, and how to do a thing called a balestra, which was a method of attacking with a little jump forward, which he rather thought they had used in *Romeo and Juliet*. He decided, quite definitely, that he was going to save up and take classes.

"Yes, why don't you?" said Anita. "You'd probably be quite good at it – seeing as you're good at ballet."

He'd temporarily forgotten about being good at ballet. He tried his best to scowl, as an indication that he would rather not be, but somehow all ill temper seemed to have evaporated. When Anita, rather wistfully, said, "It's almost four o'clock . . . I suppose we couldn't try just a *little* bit of rehearsing?" he felt an absolute heel. A whole solid hour he'd let her waste on him, even though he knew how worried she was about that second lift, which they'd never yet managed to get really right. *And* there was that bit in the middle, where he kept getting the timing wrong.

"Sorry," he said. "Didn't realize it was so late."

They rehearsed non-stop until half past six, when Mummy put her head round the door and said: "Good gracious me! Still at it? I just came to say that we're back." Now it was Anita's turn to apologize.

"Honestly," she said, "I wasn't cheating you – I didn't do it on purpose."

"Do what?" said Jamie.

"Make you stay longer than you should have. You said you had to be away by six."

"Oh! That." He grinned, rather sheepishly. "I only said that 'cos I was mad at you."

"You mean it doesn't matter?"

"Doesn't matter what time I go. Rehearse all night, if you like."

For a moment, she looked almost tempted; but then, very firmly, she shook her head.

"No. Thea always says that one reaches a cut-out point. She says if you go on too long you undo all the good work that's gone before. But if you really *don't* have to get home" – she picked up a towel and held it out to him – "then maybe you ought to stay and have dinner."

She didn't say why he ought to stay and have dinner – a reward, perhaps, for being a good boy? – but whatever the reason he wasn't averse to it.

(There's this bird I know, lives up by the golf course. One of the big houses. I was round there last Saturday, stayed on to have dinner . . .)

If Mummy and Daddy were put out to find themselves lumbered with an extra mouth at table, they were far too well bred to show it. Mummy simply opened the lid of her freezer cabinet (Jamie could hardly believe it: it was chock full of food, enough to feed an army) and said: "Right. What do we all fancy, then?" while Daddy said: "Cheers! Gives me a chance to crack a bottle", and went off to look in his wine cellar, which he kept in a cupboard under the stairs. Mrs Carr hated having people sprung on her at the last minute. She always grumbled about "not having anything in" and "not being prepared". It was one of the greatest crimes you could commit, bringing someone home without warning – except if it were Doug. She didn't care about Doug. He could just muck in with the rest of them and take pot luck. But once when Jamie had brought Sharon back she'd gone practically raving berserk. Still, he supposed it must make a difference, having a huge great freezer permanently full of food.

They talked, over the dinner table, of Anita going to ballet school. It appeared that Miss Tucker's was only a jumping-off point: as from September, she was starting full time, as a student up in London.

Mummy said: "I've warned her, time and again . . . it's a dog's life. Nothing but slave, slave, slave. And then no guarantee of ever getting anywhere. But there you are, if it's what she wants."

"It always has been," said Anita.

"Oh! It always has been. Right from the time she was a little girl. There was never any stopping her. How about you, Jamie? What are you going to do?"

He had once thought of being a professional

cricketer, but he had almost given up on that idea; especially after the last fiasco. He said he didn't know.

"You ought to try for ballet school," said Anita. "I bet they'd take you like a shot."

"For goodness' sake!" Mummy laughed, merrily, as she ground salt out of a wooden salt cellar. Jamie watched in fascination, taking careful note so that he would know how to use it if anyone said "Pass Jamie the salt". Left to himself he would simply have tilted it upside down and felt stupid when nothing came out. "There are other things in life," said Mummy, "besides ballet."

"But he's good at it," said Anita. "And they're crying out for men. They always are. There's about a thousand girls applying to every one boy."

"I'm not surprised. Boys probably have more sense."

"It isn't that. It's the fact that parents don't encourage them. Jamie's parents don't encourage *him*, do they, Jamie? His father still thinks it's a cissy thing to do. What was it you said he said? Something horrid."

Jamie muttered: "He was only joking."

"Yes, but I bet he meant it, really. I bet he thinks if you became a dancer you'd turn into some horrid mincing creature with a lisp."

Gratefully, Jamie took the salt cellar that Mummy was holding out to him and concentrated on grinding salt.

"*Honestly*," said Anita. "People are so *bigoted*."

"I wouldn't say it's bigoted, so much." Mummy reached across for another little wooden pot. "More a question of not being able to rid oneself of the ideas one's been brought up with. It's not that easy.

I daresay if *you* were a boy, we mightn't be quite so keen on the thought of your taking up ballet."

"Why not?" said Anita.

"Oh! I don't know ... I suppose because other things would seem more suitable. Pepper, Jamie? – Not that we'd stop you, of course. Any more than I daresay Jamie's father is stopping him."

"*Would* he stop you," said Anita, "if you really wanted to?"

Grind, grind, grind. First the salt, and then the pepper. He bet his mum would go crazy over it.

"Dunno," he said. "I s'pose not."

"Well, there you are, then! Why don't you?"

Why didn't he? Was she raving mad?

"Stop flogging everyone into balletomania," said Mrs Cairncross. "Some people have better things to do with their lives. What does your father do, Jamie?"

"He runs an off-licence," said Jamie.

"My God!" Daddy spoke for the first time. "There's a useful chap to know! Champagne every weekend, eh?"

Actually, it wasn't even champagne at Christmas, because Mr Carr didn't go for it. He reckoned it was overpriced. "All gas and no substance." Jamie was about to say that they occasionally had a bottle of table wine with Sunday dinner when Anita, who was not a girl to be easily deflected, broke in with: "It seems such a *waste*. When someone's really got *talent* – and anyway, what else would he do?"

Mummy said briskly: "I'm sure there are all sorts of things, aren't there, Jamie? I don't expect dancing's the only thing he's good at."

"I suppose he'll go into a *factory*," said Anita.

"Or an office," said Daddy. "Plenty of opportunities

for bright young men. What 'O' levels are you doing, Jamie?"

"History," said Jamie.

There was a pause.

"No maths?" said Daddy.

"Not much good at maths." He speared a chunk of meat with his fork. "Doing it for CSE – don't s'pose I'll pass, though."

Old Hubbard had said it would be a miracle if he scraped any marks at all. He'd said Jamie was the nearest thing he'd ever encountered to a natural born cretin – if you excepted Doug, that is. He'd said if they had a Brainless of Britain contest it would be a close run thing which of them would win.

Daddy shook his head.

"Pity," he said. "Maths is a useful thing to have."

"Why?" said Anita. "What's useful about it? So long as you can add up and subtract . . . you don't have to have *maths* to *dance*."

When he left, at nine-thirty, Anita came to the garden gate with him, smuggling his fencing foil in a cardigan. He had a sudden renewal of doubt.

"You quite sure it's OK?" he said.

"Oh, Jamie, of course I am! It's mine, isn't it? People can do what they like with their own things. If I want to give it to a friend, then I can give it to a friend . . . here!" She thrust it at him. "Take it, and don't be stupid."

He took it, holding it rigidly behind his back with one hand, in case Mummy or Daddy should be watching out of a window. He was sure, if they were, they would come running down the path to re-possess.

"If they ask you where it's gone – " he said.

"They won't. They won't know."

"But if they do – "

"I'll say I gave it away to someone who could make better use of it. You mustn't get so hung up: it's only an *object*."

"Yeah. Well – all right, then," he said. "If you're really sure."

"Jamie, I *told* you. I *said*. I said I wanted you to *have* it."

"Yeah! OK!" He stood a moment, uncertain; then awkwardly he said: "Well, I – I guess I'd better be going. Thanks a million for the supper and everything."

"Thank you for coming," said Anita. "*And* for rehearsing all that time."

"'s all right," he said.

He set off across the Common, carrying his fencing foil before him. He had just reached the first clump of trees and was about to disappear, when Anita's voice called after him: "Don't forget about tomorrow morning . . . nine o'clock sharp – and don't be late!"

10

"Hey! You! Young Carr!"

Jamie, on his way across to the field with Doug, stopped in his tracks and turned. Bob Pearson was hollering at him from a distance.

"What's his problem?" said Doug.

"Dunno."

"Tell him to get stuffed."

At any rate, he wasn't going running to him. If Bob Pearson wanted to hold a conversation, then he could shift his fat carcase and come across and do so in a civilized fashion. He wasn't going to be bawled at over half a mile of playing field.

He stood waiting. Bob Pearson, looking not best pleased, began barging his way through a flock of juniors.

"What happened, then?" He reached Jamie and glared down at him. Jamie glared back. What was he talking about, what happened? What happened when? What was he supposed to have done now?

"Friday night!" Bob Pearson spoke impatiently. "What happened?"

Friday *night*? The prickles broke out all up and down Jamie's spine. Don't say that little cow Sharon –

"There was a net practice! Four o'clock till seven! Where the devil did you get to?"

Net practice. The irony of it. And there he'd been, making up these lies – what he'd thought were lies – about "having something on at school".

"What's the matter with you? Don't you ever look at the notice board? Can't you read, or something?"

"Mental age of three," said Doug.

The Pearson ignored him.

"There's a house match next Saturday. I've got the nets booked for Tuesday and Friday. This time I want you *there*. Understood?"

"Yeah." Jamie nodded, feebly. "Sorry about last Friday. I didn't look."

"No; obviously. Well, in future make sure you do. I don't waste my time writing out lists just so people can walk past and ignore them."

"Creep," said Doug, as he went steaming off.

Later in the day, Jamie made a detour via the Assembly Hall and for the first time in weeks spared a glance at the notice board. Sure enough, there was his name: *R. Pearson* (Cap.), *D. Jones, J. Carr* –

It had been superimposed upon M. Chilvers, which had in its turn been superimposed upon A. Walker. M. Chilvers, he knew, because he had been present to witness it, had broken his wrist in the gym last Thursday. He didn't know what had happened to A. Walker. Maybe he'd been struck by lightning or got an ingrowing toenail; he didn't really care. Whatever it was, it had given him a second chance he'd never thought to have.

"Marvellous, isn't it?" said Doug, craning over his shoulder. "Expects you to come crawling back the minute he crooks his little finger . . . even has the diabolical nerve to yell at you for not keeping an eye on his poxy notice board. What's he think you're going to do? Chase up and down every five minutes looking at the flaming thing?"

It hadn't struck Jamie that way – he'd just been happy to find himself with a second chance. Doug was quite right, though. He tried to instil some indignation into himself.

"Know what I'd do?" said Doug. "I'd tell him to stuff his lousy house match right up his – "

"Yeah, I know," said Jamie. It was easy enough for Doug to say what he would do: Doug didn't have these dreams of being a professional cricketer. There wasn't any point in cutting off one's nose to spite one's face. "I'll tell you one thing," he said. "He's not getting me run out again. No way. He tries any funny business, he's the one going to end up with egg on his face."

The picture of Bob Pearson with egg on his face was a pleasurable one: it solaced him for any feeling of weakness he might have for allowing himself to be put upon.

"Matter of interest," said Doug, "what *were* you doing on Friday? Someone said they saw you with Sharon down the Folk Club."

"Don't talk to me about that place," said Jamie. "And don't talk to me about Sharon, either. I've had it with that girl."

"Not before time," said Doug. "I always told you you wouldn't get anywhere with her."

"*You* always told me? *You* always told me – " He stopped. What was the point? It didn't matter any more, what Doug had always told him. Maybe Doug didn't know quite as much about girls as they'd both thought he did. "Anyway," he said, carelessly, "I've got someone else."

"Who's that, then? Not old kinky Coral?"

"Nope." He couldn't resist just a little bit of boasting. "Doesn't go to Tenterden. Goes to the High."

"Cor!" said Doug, playing awestruck. "Mixing with the nobs! You wait till she takes you home to meet Mummy and Daddy ... it'll be round the servants' entrance for you, mate."

"I've already been home with her," said Jamie. "Had dinner round there, Saturday."

"Dinner already!" Doug's tone was jeering, but he looked at Jamie with what seemed a new respect. As they parted company at the school gates, he said: "You going to bring this new bird down the disco sometime, then?"

"Might do," said Jamie.

He wondered, on his way home ... if Anita were to hear herself described as "his bird", would she be indignant? Or did she now regard herself as in any sense belonging to him?

After some hesitation, when he got in, he looked up Cairncross in the telephone book. After more hesitation – quite a lot more, as a matter of fact: it took him a full half hour of dithering before he could nerve himself – he picked up the receiver and dialled the number. It was Mummy who answered. She sounded quite friendly. She said: "Hallo, Jamie. Do you want Anita? I'll get her for you." And then he heard her shouting: "Anita! There's Jamie on the telephone." After a few seconds, Anita's voice came, breathlessly: "Jamie? Oh, Jamie, you're *not* going to say you can't make it on Wednesday?"

"No," he said. "I was just ringing to find out if you were doing anything tonight?"

"Tonight?" She didn't seem to think it odd of him, or presumptuous. She seemed to think it quite natural. She said: "Actually, I'm going up to Bird-hurst Park to watch the Morris dancing."

Jamie said: "Oh."

"I'm going with a girl from school . . . you could always come with us if you wanted."

He might have done had it been Anita by herself, but not even for the sake of calling her his bird was he prepared to spend an evening watching Morris dancing in company with her and a girl friend. Men in tights was one thing: men with little bells on their ankles was more than he could take. He wasn't getting dragged into *that* scene. He asked her what about tomorrow, but tomorrow, it seemed, she had a class. She had classes Tuesdays, Wednesdays, Thursdays and Fridays – not to mention rehearsing all afternoon every Saturday. She was stark mad; not a doubt of it. He arranged that he would go and pick her up on Wednesday, so they could walk over the Common together to Miss Tucker's. He supposed that that was better than nothing.

He went round early on Wednesday, as soon as tea was finished. His mother had insisted he carry a bottle of wine with him, to make up for having stayed to dinner on Saturday. He'd done his best to wangle champagne, but she hadn't taken the hint, so now he was stuck with an end-of-bin Beaujolais, which he had a horrid feeling was probably the sort of wine that Mrs Cairncross used for cooking in. He was in two minds whether to ditch the thing before he got there, but then he had visions of his mother seeking out Anita's mother at the fearful fiasco that Miss Tucker would insist on calling "a divertissement" and asking her how she'd liked the wine, so he gritted his teeth and hung on to it. It was Daddy he handed it over to. Daddy said: "Oh! A bottle of plonk! How perfectly splendid – this year's vintage, too," which made it sound as if maybe it was all right after all.

Anita was in her school uniform. He'd never seen

120

her in it before. It was salmon pink: a salmon pink dress, buttoned all the way down the front, with white collar and cuffs. It was the sort of dress that his Mum would have liked Kim to wear – all neat and tidy and little-girlish. It ought by rights to have reduced its wearer very firmly to the status of a schoolgirl. Instead, it made her look almost grown up. It made him feel quite gauche and clodhopping – possibly because he *was* gauche and clodhopping. Gauche and clodhopping and only taking one "O" level. He bet she wouldn't even look twice at him if it weren't for the fact that she needed him for her precious ballet. Probably wouldn't be seen *dead* with him. He wished there were something he could do that would impress her.

On their way to Miss Tucker's, across the Common, they came upon a gang of little kids from Jamie's street messing about with a bat and a ball, using a tree trunk with chalk marks for a wicket. If he'd been by himself they'd have clamoured at him to join in: because he was with a girl, and a girl whom none of them recognized, they obviously felt too shy. Magnanimously, he joined in anyway. This was his chance – the very chance he'd been waiting for. At least he would show her there was *some*thing he could do.

"Hang on a sec." He snapped his fingers for the bat, took up his stance at the tree-trunk wicket, called casually down the pitch to Luke Gibbs, who was in the same class as Kim, to "Toss us one up, then." Luke obliged. Fortunately he could bowl better than some of the kids: it was at any rate reasonably on course. With an air of satisfaction, Jamie stepped forward, opened up his shoulders and sent it smacking out through the covers for six. The crack of the bat meeting ball was music. Even if

Anita knew nothing whatsoever of cricket, she could hardly fail to have recognized it as a classic stroke.

He stood back, smiling and benevolent: the professional cricketer surrounded by his admirers. One of the little kids had gone scampering after the ball. He picked it up, and in his excitement hurled it back towards the wicket. Jamie, reaching out a careless hand to arrest its flight, found himself suddenly attacked by a screeching virago.

"*Jamie!* Your *hands!*"

All the little kids stopped and stared. (He could just hear them, afterwards, amongst themselves: *Jamie!* Your *hands!*) Playing it cool, he tossed the ball back to the bowler, surrendered his bat and allowed himself to be dragged off. The minute they were out of earshot, he turned on her.

"What was that for?"

"Your *hands!*" She almost screamed it at him. "That was a hard ball . . . you could have broken something!"

He looked at her stolidly.

"So what?"

"So you've got to *dance* on Saturday! You've got to *partner* me!"

"Is that all you ever think about?" he said. "Dancing?"

"No, of course it isn't! But just at this *moment* – "

"So what else do you ever think about?" he said.

"Lots of things! Loads of things!"

"Tell me some."

"*Tell* you some?" It was the first time he had ever seen her at all disconcerted. "Well – "

"Do you ever think about the Bomb and people starving and what it's like not to have money?"

"Yes – sometimes."

"You mean like about once in every blue moon?"

122

She rallied slightly.

"Well, how often do you?"

"More than you, I bet. Do you know, I've never heard you talk about anything that wasn't ballet?"

A slight pinkness invaded her cheek. He noted it with satisfaction. Others before him, he thought, had had cause to complain.

"It's not that I'm not interested in other things." She said it earnestly, as if trying to convince herself as much as him. "It's just that when you want to do something like ballet there simply isn't *room* for anything else. If you want to get anywhere, you really have to dedicate yourself."

"Crap," said Jamie.

That took her aback – he bet no one had ever said crap to her in the whole of her pampered life.

"Jamie, it isn't crap!" she said. "It's true! There's only one way you can ever hope to achieve anything, and that's by being completely single-minded. Imagine if you wanted to be a footballer, or a boxer, or a – a pop star, or something." That's right, he thought. Bring it down to my level. Something that a common boy from Tenterden Road Comprehensive might just about be able to grasp. "Imagine how hard you'd have to work," said Anita. "Imagine all the training sessions and the practice. Well, it's exactly the same with dancing. It's just no *use* thinking you can skip class every time you're a bit off colour or something a bit more interesting happens to turn up." (Was that a dig at him?) "It's no *use* thinking you can play football or cricket or do things that are going to develop muscles in all the wrong places. You have to put the ballet first."

"That's if you're going to be a dancer," he said.

"And you're not?" She shot a quick glance at him.

"Did you think any more about that? About what I said? I'm sure that if you tried for a ballet school – "

"I'm not trying for any ballet school!" His tone was tetchy: he could hear that it was. "My old man would have a fit."

"Is that the only thing that stops you?"

"No, it is not!" Whoever heard of a boy from Tenterden Road Comprehensive going to a ballet school? It was a ludicrous idea. Imagine standing up in a careers class and saying, "Please, sir, I'm going to ballet school." Doug would die laughing.

"You mean," said Anita, "that you would honestly rather spend the rest of your life doing some boring, soulless job in a factory than being a dancer?"

Why did she automatically assume that it had to be a factory?

Because he went to Tenterden Road Comprehensive and was only taking one "O" level, that was why.

He said: "I'm not going into a factory."

"Well, all right, an office, then! It's all the same – it's all boring and soulless. If you're not minding machines you're sitting at a desk writing letters. And you'd rather do that than *dance*?"

"I'm not going to do that," he said.

"So what are you going to do?"

There were a million things he could do. He could join the army and learn how to kill people – he could join the police and harass all the black kids – he could run an off-licence and hump beer crates about –

"I'm going to play cricket," he said. "And what's more, I'm going to play it on Saturday."

"*Saturday?*" Her voice rose, shrilly. "But that's the day of the show!"

He enjoyed seeing her all out of control – she who as a rule was so cool and calm and superior.

"I know it is," he said.

"Then how can you possibly play cricket?"

"It's all right," he said. "You don't have to panic." (Privately, he thought it might do her good just for once.) "The match is in the morning – it'll be over by two. Gives me bags of time. Show doesn't start till seven-thirty."

"But your hands!" She screamed it at him. "What about your *hands*?"

"What about them?" he said. "I'm not a flaming concert pianist."

"Jamie, I know you think I'm making an absurd amount of fuss, but honestly – " she looked at him, pleading – "honestly, I'm *not*. I'm really *not*. You've only got to have the slightest of sprains, or pull a muscle, or even just bruise yourself – "

"So what are you suggesting? I should wear a suit of armour?"

She bit her lip.

"Surely they could find somebody else? Just for this once?"

He was very certain they could; all too easily. And it wouldn't be just for this once.

"I'm not stopping playing cricket only for some lousy ballet show," he said.

"Jamie! That's not fair!"

"It is fair."

It was fair. Think of all the Saturday afternoons he'd sacrificed – all the Sunday mornings, all the Wednesdays and Fridays. It was most certainly fair.

In a low, intense voice, Anita said: "You don't seem to realize how important this is."

Didn't realize how important it was? He was sick

to death of being *told* how important it was. Come to that, he was sick to death of the whole thing.

"If anything were to happen and you couldn't dance – "

"Then you'd have to make do with Garstin, wouldn't you?"

Her chin went up.

"I wouldn't dance with Garstin if he were the last man left on earth! I wouldn't be seen dead on the same stage with Garstin!"

Such exaggerated over-reaction irritated him.

"Well, that's your problem," he said. "I can't guarantee I'm not going to be knocked stone cold. It's a chance you have to take."

Anita, very pale, said: "You mean, you're going to go ahead and play?"

She'd better believe it.

"Furthermore," he said – the word sounded good, so he said it again: "Furthermore, I don't even know for sure whether I'm going to be able to make the dress rehearsal Friday. We've got a net practice goes on till seven. If it ends on time I might be able to get there for half past. All depends how the light holds. Sometimes these things run over – might be nearer eight."

Anita didn't say "Oh, but Jamie, you *must*" – she didn't even bother saying her usual "*Please*, Jamie." Maybe she was tired of it. Or maybe she guessed that in his present mood it would be a waste of breath. He'd been pushed far enough, he wasn't being pushed any further. Quietly, in a voice devoid of expression, she said: "You'd better tell Miss Tucker."

He didn't, of course. When it came to it, he couldn't. However mad Anita might make him, he just could never work himself up to the same pitch

126

of indignation against Miss Tucker. When she went yum-pumming about the room ("*Yum*-pum! *Yum*-pum! *Yum*-pum!") he wanted to laugh, but at the same time he wanted to join in, he wanted to do things that would please her. When she patted him on the head and said "Good boy!" or "Well done!" he didn't writhe and cringe as he would if anyone else had dared to take the liberty. She made him feel about three years old, but somehow he didn't mind. It amused him to humour her – and yet her praise, when it came, was very sweet. He decided he would tell Bob Pearson that he could only stay till five-thirty on Friday. When all was said and done, it was Miss Tucker who'd got in first. She ought, in fairness, to have priority.

He approached the Pearson on Tuesday, during a break in practice. Fortunately he was on form – he'd just been slamming the bowling right and left, even the great Pearson had been moved to murmur words of approval – so he reckoned it wasn't such a bad moment to ask.

"Will it be OK," he said, "if I leave at five-thirty on Friday?"

"No, it will not be OK!" The Pearson looked at him with the same irritation with which Jamie had looked at Anita. "You need all the practice you can get. You already missed out on last Friday."

"I wouldn't have done if I'd known. I didn't know that you wanted me."

"So whose fault was that? You should have kept an eye on the notice board, like you're supposed to. You found out quick enough when you were selected for the team!"

"Yeah, I just can't get used to the five-minute updates."

"Button it, smart arse! You're either interested in what goes on, or you're not."

"I am!"

"So what's with this sloping off early on Friday?"

"It's just that I promised somebody. Ages ago. I promised I'd do something."

"Well, if it's some bird you were thinking of taking somewhere, you can forget it."

"It isn't a bird."

"So what is it, then?"

He was damned if he was going to tell a creep like Bob Pearson what it was. (Please, I have to rehearse for a divertissement . . .) Defiantly, he said: "It's helping out with a show. For spastics."

"On Friday evening?"

"Yeah – well, that's when the dress rehearsal is. I told them that I'd be there."

"You told them that you'd be there on a Friday evening? When you know perfectly bloody well that nine times out of ten Friday evenings are when net practices are held? Well, I'm sorry! I don't have people on my team with divided loyalties. To me, the House comes first. That's the way I expect it to be for everyone else. If it's not, then I'm not interested. You either play cricket, or you go off and do this other thing. It's up to you. You're going to have to choose."

"But it's for *spastics*," said Jamie.

"I don't give a toss what it's for! It could be for snow-blind huskies, for all I care. I've got a job to do, getting a team together. Like I said, you either want to be part of it or you don't; it's as simple as that. If you do, then you turn up on Friday and you stay till the end the same as everyone else. If you don't, you'd better tell me now, so that I can make other arrangements."

He wondered, glumly, what the other arrangements would be. There was a kid in Class 4 who was said to be pretty hot stuff – for a kid. A fourteen-year-old taking his place! It would be more than he could bear.

"Well, come on!" The Pearson tapped impatiently with his bat on the coconut matting. "Which is it to be? Us or Them? I haven't got all day."

Desperately, Jamie said: "I just don't like having to let people down."

"Which people?"

"Well . . . *them*."

"I see." The Pearson nodded, coldly. "You don't mind letting the House down: that doesn't bother you."

"Yes, it does!" (Actually, it didn't. The only thing that bothered him was losing his place on the team.) "It does, but they're spastics!"

"Well, unless you can perform a miracle and be in two places at the same time, you can forget it." The Pearson turned away, in disgust. "You're the sort that would sell his country down the drain in time of war. People like you I can do without. You needn't bother looking at the notice board any more: your name certainly won't be appearing there."

He thought, afterwards, of a thousand retorts he might have made. He might have told the Pearson, for a start, that it was dumb clods like him that caused wars in the first place – all this Us and Them business. All this junk about the House coming first. The guy was a throwback. He wouldn't be at all surprised if he belonged to the National Front. It was just the sort of fascist organization that would appeal to one of his blinkered mentality. Of course, at the time, he couldn't think of a single thing to say other than "Look, I'm *sorry* – " which now he would have given anything not to have said. The Pearson hadn't taken a blind bit of notice. It had just been demeaning himself for no purpose.

He didn't even receive from Doug the sympathy he might have looked for. Doug, whilst not subscribing to the "House first, last and always" business, nevertheless seemed to think he was raving mad. Putting some crummy dancing show before a cricket match?

"I wouldn't normally," said Jamie. "But when you've actually *promised* someone – "

He couldn't help feeling there'd been a bit of a change in Doug's attitude from earlier in the week, when he'd been all for telling the Pearson to "stuff his lousy cricket match". Now he wanted him to tell little old Miss Tucker to stuff her lousy dancing show. He just couldn't do it; not even for a place on the team. If he didn't arrive on time Friday evening it would louse everything up for her. She needed him there right from the beginning. She'd gone and put in this opening number (she called it a "Grande Parade", pronounced Grond Parahd) where everyone had to come on and form themselves into a sort of avenue, and then he and Anita were going to appear in a spotlight and he was going to lead her down to the front of the stage and all the audience (hopefully) were going to look at them and think what a beautiful picture they made. He supposed, for Anita, it was a big moment. Not that it was for Anita he was doing it: it was for little old Miss Tucker, so that she could sit back and be happy.

As a matter of fact, he wasn't feeling very kindly disposed towards Anita just at this moment. He hadn't forgotten about the fencing foil, but the more he thought about it the more he felt certain she'd only given it to him as a means of keeping him sweet. It wasn't because she liked him, or thought him in any way special. She probably didn't like him. She probably thought he was an uncultured lout. Good enough to dance with, but definitely not One of Us. If only, just once, she would give some sign of appreciating him as a person. Even *acknowledging* him as a person. He didn't want her to fawn. He didn't want her prostrating herself, or anything like that. It was just that every now and again he had this corny vision of her throwing her arms about his neck. He knew it was corny. It was so corny it almost made him want to bring up. So why did he keep thinking of it? She wasn't going to do it. He couldn't imagine Anita ever doing it to anyone.

11

Friday evening, he walked over the Common with Kim, who prattled the entire way about the costumes she was going to wear. She didn't only have her Dewdrop costume, but her Russian costume and her Peasant costume, as well. Anyone would think, thought Jamie, that it was a fashion show she was appearing in.

She wanted to know what his costumes were like. He said sternly, to discourage such frivolity, that he couldn't remember; which actually wasn't true, since he could remember all too well. He had spent half the session on Wednesday being pinned into things by Miss Harrell and paraded for inspection before Miss Tucker. The Russian get-up hadn't been too bad – at any rate, he didn't feel quite such a fool in it as he'd thought he was going to – but the other had been a decided embarrassment. Nobody had told him that the tights were going to be *white* (somehow he'd had it settled in his mind that they would be black: black, and very thick) and the long tunic that he'd been promised wasn't long at all, it hardly came down as far as his hips. He'd asked if it wasn't a bit on the small side, but Miss Harrell had seemed surprised and said that on the contrary, it couldn't have fitted better: "You must be about exactly the same size as David." Hopefully, he'd tried suggesting that maybe he was *taller* than David – maybe the tunic ought to be a bit *longer* – but Miss Harrell had pooh-poohed the idea.

"It would ruin the line. Besides, it wouldn't be as comfortable."

He'd nearly said that it could hardly be a question of its being *as* comfortable, since the way it was at the moment it wasn't comfortable at all, but he'd ended up just suffering in silence, with the result that he was now faced with the hideous prospect of actually having to be *seen* in the thing.

The Church Hall, when they arrived, was pandemonium. All the Dewdrops were running about shrieking – "Miss Tucker, I can't find my *shoes*!" "Miss Tucker, someone's stolen my *head*band!" "Miss Tucker, Andrea's going to be *sick*!" Garstin was complaining to anyone who would listen, only no one had the time to do so, that he couldn't possibly wear the costume he'd been given because it had been sewn with nylon thread and he was allergic to nylon thread. A couple of mothers who'd come in to help with wardrobe were trying unsuccessfully to round up the Dewdrops and put them all in one place. Even Miss Tucker was not her usual calm, brisk self but showed a tendency towards shouting and flying about. The only people who remained cool, so far as he could see, were himself, Miss Harrell, and a stray father who had volunteered to work the lights. He didn't know where Anita was. He assumed she must be there, but if so she was keeping herself well hidden. Miss Tucker flashed past him, going like the Red Queen. She patted him briefly on the head with a "That's right! Good boy! Go and get into your costume. Anita will come and make you up presently."

He wasn't sure that he fancied the idea of Anita

making him up; not after their last interchange. He wasn't sure that he fancied the idea of getting into his costume. He had to share a poky cupboard with Garstin, who was still fretfully complaining about his allergy to nylon thread.

"It's always the same. You buy things that say hundred per cent cotton and then you find they've gone and stitched them up with nylon. That's what's happened here. It's absolutely useless. I shall be itching all evening."

Jamie had never spoken very much to Garstin before. He didn't particularly want to speak to him now, but in fact, apart from his obsession with the nylon thread, he turned out to be quite reasonable. The way Anita carried on, you'd think he was a complete dead loss. He understood about cricket, however, and he supported Surrey, so he couldn't be all that bad. Furthermore, he knew that he was hopeless when it came to anything physical. The only reason he'd come to Miss Tucker's, he said, was because he'd thought she did ballroom dancing. He'd wanted to learn ballroom dancing so that he could go in for competitions and meet girls. Then he'd found she only did ballet, and he'd thought that perhaps that would be even better – from the point of view of meeting girls, that is. He'd reckoned there wouldn't be much in the way of competition; not in a ballet school.

"And there wasn't," he said. "Well, I mean, apart from David, and he wouldn't have known what to do with a girl if he got one. Of course, they were all potty over him. Girls always go potty over his sort. Actually, you're a bit like him. They'll probably go potty over you pretty soon."

Jamie shot him a hard look, but he seemed to have made the remark quite innocently. Garstin, he decided, was one of nature's babblers. Harmless enough; but a babbler.

"I've got to go and get made up," he said at last, somewhat to Jamie's relief. "Miss Harrell's going to do me. Anita won't. I get on her nerves."

"Was Anita potty over David?" said Jamie.

"Anita doesn't go potty over people," said Garstin. "David said she was a cold fish."

He thought about it as he tugged at his tunic, trying in vain to stretch it further down over his hips. He didn't think Anita was a cold fish, exactly. She wasn't cold to dance with, and she wasn't cold when she was talking about ballet. She became almost animated then. If she could only become animated about something *other* than ballet, she would be really quite a nice person to know. After all, she did have her good points. She wasn't mean or spiteful or petty-minded; not like Sharon. She almost never lost her temper or took offence – and after all, she had given him a fencing foil. Whatever her motives, it was still a pretty generous thing to have done. It was just a pity she was so one-track minded. It sometimes made it very difficult not to feel impatient with her.

He had just given up on the tunic (mainly for fear the material would rip if he tugged at it any longer) when there was a tap at the door and there she was. She was wearing a sort of wrapper thing, and her eyes were all done into fantastic shapes, with long lines sweeping out from the corners.

"I've come to do your make-up," she said.

She didn't smile at him or say "Thank you for being here" or "I knew you wouldn't let us down", or indeed give any indication at all that she was prepared to forgive and forget. If she had, he would have told her about not playing cricket tomorrow; but as she didn't, neither did he.

They hardly talked at all as she smeared make-up over his face. Jamie ventured the odd remark about "Miss Tucker being all of a flap" and "Garstin threatening to break out into a rash", but Anita only pursed her lips and smiled rather distantly. He wondered if she was sulking over what had happened on Wednesday. He wouldn't have thought she was the type, but maybe him saying "crap" had upset her more than he'd realized. Maybe she'd come to the conclusion that he was just a yob, and that she couldn't be bothered with him any more. Well, that was all right by him. After tomorrow, she wouldn't have to be.

That evening, for the first time, he met the great David. He knew at once who it was when he saw a youth with his arm in a sling standing next to Miss Tucker, talking with her, all matey-matey, as if on equal terms. He felt a momentary stirring of what might almost have been jealousy, except that that was patently absurd, because what was there to be jealous about? *He* didn't want to compete. Miss Tucker suddenly broke off her conversation and went scuttling away, with her dancer's ducklike waddle, to correct someone's port de bras (he'd learnt all the posh French names by now) or shove someone back into line. The youth slowly turned, and his eye fell upon Jamie.

"So you're the prodigy?" he said. "I've been hearing great and wonderful things about you."

"I got pressganged," said Jamie. "You want to take over again, you're quite welcome."

The youth curled his lip slightly. Other than being of roughly the same height and build, Jamie totally failed to see any resemblance to himself. Simply because they both had dark hair and brown eyes, that didn't make them the same, did it?

"I fancy it's just as well," said the youth, "that I can't take you up on that offer. I might not find myself welcomed back with quite the rapturous enthusiasm you seem to think. At any rate, I'd rather not have to put it to the test . . . from all accounts, my son, you're something of a budding Nijinsky."

Jamie scowled, suspecting sarcasm. In any case, he didn't want to be a budding Nijinsky. If he was going to be a budding anything, he'd rather it was a budding Botham.

"True as I stand here," said David, "Thea's just been singing your praises. If your ears aren't burning, they jolly well ought to be." His ears weren't, but his cheeks were starting to. "I tell you, she's falling over herself . . . I gather you're what's known as a natural – don't need to be taught like the rest of us. Lucky feller." He winked. "They'll be doing *Spectre de la Rose* next, just so you can leap through the window."

"There isn't going to be any next," said Jamie. He didn't know anything about *Spectre de la Rose*, whatever that was, but he did know that *he* wasn't going to be doing any leaping about in it. "I'm only helping them out this once. Just until you come back."

David said: "Don't you kid yourself! Once Thea gets her hands on a bit of talent, she doesn't let go that easily. In any case, sorry to disappoint you, but I won't be coming back. That's what I came to tell Thea – in case she was missing me, which obviously she isn't. I've got a place at the Arts Educational. Starting next September. As far as I'm concerned, the field's all yours."

"Thanks very much," said Jamie, playing the heavy sarcasm bit.

"Oh, don't mention it! Only too glad I'm not going to be around – don't think I could take the competition. Not at my age. Not from a budding Nijinsky. Mind you" – he smiled, amiably – "I personally shall reserve judgement until I've seen you in the Borodin . . . seeing as Thea wrote that specially for me. She tells me she's had to modify it slightly – but only slightly. I shall be interested to see what you do with it."

See if I fall flat on my face, thought Jamie. After all, it was no more than he would be hoping for, in David's position.

David's smile increased: it was as if he knew exactly what thoughts were going through Jamie's head.

"I'll let you know what I think of it," he said.

He didn't really care two straws what David thought of it; not really. He wouldn't have had a sleepless night if the guy had come backstage afterwards and made some snide remark. On the other hand, when he looked round the door and said "Hey, Nijinsky! That was bloody good!" he couldn't help warming to him. Not so much because he'd thought it was good, but because he'd actually come and told him so. That took some doing, Jamie knew. If whoever replaced him in the match tomorrow turned out to be a hero, he wasn't at all sure that he would be able to bring himself to go and offer congratulations.

Shortly after David, Anita turned up. She put her head round the door and said: "Thank goodness for that . . . he's gone." He thought at first she was referring to David, but quickly realized that she meant Garstin. "Daddy's coming in the car to pick me up," she said. "Would you and Kim like a lift?"

He might almost have been tempted to decline (considering she'd said scarcely a word to him all evening) except that last Wednesday, when he'd gone to collect her, he'd seen Daddy's car standing in the drive, a big new Jaguar XJS: it was more than he could resist.

"Sure, OK," he said. "Thanks." He said it as offhandedly as he could – to his ears, it sounded suitably ungracious. Anita, however, didn't seem to notice.

"Shall I take your make-up off?" she said. "You look as if you're making an awful mess. I'm sorry, by the way" – determinedly, she removed the greasy lump of cotton wool with which he had been daubing at his face and threw it in the waste bin – "I'm sorry if I've seemed a bit standoffish. I haven't meant to be. It's just that I always get absolutely paralysed before a performance – even when it's only a dress rehearsal. I'm all right once I'm actually on stage. It's all that hanging about beforehand. I get so wound up I feel I shall be sick if I even so much as open my mouth."

"That's OK," he said. Now he felt a louse. Really, she *wasn't* such a bad sort of girl. He grinned. "I expect I'd have been too scared to talk to you, anyway."

She looked at him, sympathetically.

"Did *you* get nervous?"

"Not of dancing," he said. "Of you."

"Nervous of *me*?"

"In all that gear." He'd seen her in a ballet dress often enough (Kim said he ought to call it a tutu, not a ballet dress, but he couldn't bring himself to do it: it sounded too stupid) but the one she wore to practise in was just some old, limp, floppy thing, rather like his Gran's lace curtains. The one she'd had on tonight had been all crisp and foaming, layer upon layer of net, with a stiff satin bodice which made it look as if she'd really got something there. He wouldn't have said it before, but he didn't mind saying it now: "You looked" – he was about to say "pretty good", but at the last minute he substituted "smashing" instead – "you looked smashing," he said.

"Did I?" A blush appeared on her cheek. "You looked super in the Borodin. Really fierce. And d'you know what Marjorie said when she saw you in the second half?"

"Cor blimey look at them legs?" said Jamie.

Anita laughed.

"Actually, no . . . she said, *that boy has a decided touch of the Michael Somes.*"

Jamie clapped a hand to his head.

"So that's what it is! I've been feeling a bit peculiar all evening. What do I have to do to get rid of it?"

"Nothing, if you've got any sense. Michael Somes used to partner Fonteyn. They were famous. I think secretly he must have been one of Marjorie's childhood idols . . . she's always saying how Michael *Somes* did things, or how Michael *Somes* looked in the part. It's about the highest compliment she could pay you, saying you've got a touch of him."

"Cripes," said Jamie, imitating Doug.

"Well, she never said it about David," said Anita, "and *he* was the cat's whiskers – until you turned up. You ought to be flattered. Aren't you, just a little?" She eyed him, curiously, through the dressing-table mirror. "I know you *pretend* not to care, but surely it's nice to be good at things?"

140

"I suppose so," he said; and then, after a moment's struggle: "You can relax about tomorrow, by the way. The cricket's off."

"You mean it's been cancelled?"

"No," he said. "I mean I've gone and got thrown out."

She glanced at him with swift concern.

"Not because of this evening?"

"It was either coming here to rehearse, or staying there to practise. They said I'd got to choose."

"Oh!" For just a second, he thought she might almost be going to throw her arms about him and say how glad she was that he'd chosen to come and rehearse; but then, reaching out for some cotton wool, she said: "Well, I'm sorry, and I think it's absolutely rotten of them, but you mustn't feel too badly about it . . . one has to keep these things in proportion. After all" – she cupped a hand beneath his chin, tilting his head back towards her – "it is only a game, isn't it?"

12

He didn't want to go and watch the interhouse cricket match on Saturday. The only reason he forced himself into it was because on balance he thought it would probably look better than if he stayed away. If he stayed away people might think he just couldn't take it: by turning up he was demonstrating to all and sundry that he really couldn't care less. After all, as Anita had said, it was only a game, wasn't it?

It may have been only a game: that didn't stop it being agony. Every nerve in his body twitched and writhed with the desire to pick up a bat and go marching out there. The pain of not being able to do so was almost a physical one. It didn't help that people kept coming up to him and saying "Why aren't you playing?" and "Why have they put that kid in instead of you?" The only thing that helped was that "that kid" was clean bowled before he'd even had a chance to score. Jamie strolled across and commiserated with him, and for a moment felt pretty good, but then that idiot Doug had to go and ruin it all by prophesying glumly that "We're probably going to lose, now. Thanks to you and that stupid show. If you'd been playing, you'd never have got out to a ball like that." He was glad Doug had such faith in his ability, but at the same time he couldn't help feeling a faint twinge of irritation.

"You were the one that said I ought to tell him what he could do with his lousy house match," he said.

"Figure of speech," said Doug. "Not meant to be taken literally."

"Oh, yes?" said Jamie.

As they were leaving the field (the House having been duly beaten up four wickets and Bob Pearson looking like someone who'd just downed half a pint of sour beer) Jamie felt a prod in the ribs, at the same time as a high falsetto voice screeched in his ear: "*Ja*mie! Your *hands*!" Spinning round, he encountered a baboon-like face split by a mocking leer. Another voice called from behind, in jeering echo: "Hey, Jamie . . . what about your hands?" At this, Doug spun round as well.

"What's your problem, Roy Canary?"

Roy Canary (his name was actually Canaris. They called him Canary just to rile him) made a gesture with two fingers.

"Who pulled your string?"

Doug clenched his fists. Jamie could see that he was about to take a swing – knew that if Doug took a swing, they would both become involved – grabbed him by the arm and hauled him out of temptation's reach.

"Leave 'em. They're not worth it."

He was not as a rule averse to a scrap, but somehow he didn't reckon Miss Tucker would be too pleased if he were to turn up this evening with a black eye or a cut lip. Baboon Face, grinning, came dancing round in front of them. He flapped his hands, limp-wristed, in Jamie's face.

"Who doesn't want to hurt his puddy wuddies, 'en?"

Jamie took a deep breath. His fists, involuntarily, bunched themselves up. He could feel his muscles tensing, ready for action. Another crack like that –

"Who's afwaid the nasty hard ball might bweak his ickle wists?"

Just in time, he thought of Anita. Slowly – very slowly – he uncurled his fingers.

"Twist off, sunshine! You're not amusing anyone."

He turned on his heel. He didn't care whether Doug was coming or not. There was a limit to the amount he could be expected to take, even for Anita's sake – even for Miss Tucker's. A second longer and he wouldn't answer for the consequences: a punch-up would be inevitable.

He heard Doug's voice, shouting a final obscenity; then, as he caught up with Jamie: "What was all that about?"

"I dunno. Their idea of a joke, I s'pose. Because I wasn't playing."

Doug, belligerent, said: "Why don't we go back and work 'em over?"

"Not worth all the aggro. Not for those morons."

"You mean you're going to let them get away with it?"

"Blokes like that are so thick," said Jamie, "you could mash 'em to a pulp and you still wouldn't reach grey matter."

"I don't want to reach grey matter! I just want to give 'em a pasting."

"No, you don't," said Jamie. "It'd demean you."

Doug subsided, muttering. He plainly wasn't happy about it; neither was Jamie, if it came to that. He wondered if Anita would ever appreciate just how much it had cost him, not to lay one on

144

that grinning ape – he wondered how the grinning ape had ever come to hear of the incident in the first place. He was in 5 Remedial, Jamie couldn't remember what his name was (if, indeed, he had ever known it) but he had an uncomfortable feeling that at some time or another he'd seen both him and Roy Canary knocking about with Luke Gibbs and the other kids. If they'd got hold of the story, it would be all round Class 5 in next to no time. *Hell*.

He kicked angrily at a stone. He'd got Anita to thank for that – her and her precious ballet. Nothing else mattered, did it? One-track bloody mind. Just so long as she could dance, everyone else could go hang. On the other hand –

On the other hand, she really *wasn't* such a bad sort. His bitterness against her subsided slightly. Anita was OK – and anyway, he reckoned he owed her. She'd not only given him that fencing foil, but in spite of all his moaning she'd shown him that there was at least *one* thing in life he could do better than other people. He guessed that was pretty important. At any rate, it was more important than a couple of bug-eyed morons trying to be funny. If word got out, he could always make up some story. He could always say he'd got this new bird had had a relative died of brittle bones (his great grand-dad had died of brittle bones).

"Every time she sees a cricket ball it makes her think of him. Gets her all upset . . ."

Some sort of guff. They'd swallow anything, if you told it with enough conviction.

"That Canary," said Doug. He said it in tones of deep loathing. "That Canary's got it coming to him."

Jamie suddenly cheered up.

"Monday," he said. Monday he could get as many black eyes, bruise as many knuckles, as he liked.

145

"Any more lip on Monday, and we let 'em have it. Right?"

"You've got it," said Doug.

The curtain went up strictly on time: seven-thirty to the very dot. Jamie, standing in the spotlight with Anita, on the high rostrum at the back of the stage, awaiting the moment when he must lead her down the steps, through the avenue of assorted Dewdrops and others, felt himself suddenly exposed to the critical gaze of a couple of hundred pairs of eyes and experienced a rush of pure panic. He had never realized it was going to be like this. Last night, at the dress rehearsal, it had been quite different. There hadn't been anyone out there then, save David and Miss Tucker and a small handful of parents. Now the place was jam-packed. Row upon row of upturned faces, bobbing whitely before him in the darkness like a field full of giant turnips. And all of them looking at *him* – or so it seemed. His throat grew dry, his tongue grew furry, his palms broke out into a cold sweat. Could this be stage fright?

Anita's hand felt for his and squeezed it, reassuringly. He remembered that Anita was all right once she was on stage. It was only beforehand that she became paralysed. Obviously, for him, it was the other way round. He was grateful for the physical contact, but he didn't know what good it was going to do him. His legs had turned to semolina pudding, all wobbly and uncertain. He'd never be able to get them downstage, and even if he did he couldn't remember what he was supposed to do with them. Every single step that Miss Tucker had taught him had gone – completely vanished – from his mind. Jesus! That was their cue!

Somehow (he afterwards had no recollection of it)

146

he got down the steps and through the avenue. His legs, for all that they had turned to semolina pudding, must have taken over automatically from his brain, for when at last he came to his senses it was to find them carrying him about the stage of their own accord, faithfully executing all those steps which his conscious mind had rejected. He knew, then, that it was going to be all right. He didn't have to keep torturing himself with "What comes next?" or "What do I do after this?" He need only trust to his legs and they would do it for him.

From that moment, he began to enjoy himself. By the time the Borodin was reached, at the end of the first half, he was feeling positively jubilant. A sort of exhilaration swept over him: almost a sense of power. He was up here, dancing, and they were down there, watching. *They* were watching *him*. It really was him, now. It couldn't be anyone else, because for just a few breath-taking seconds he had the stage all to himself. Tchum *da* dum, tchum *da* dum, tchum *da* dum – BAM! It felt good, it felt terrific, it could go on all night. He saw what it was that Anita got out of it. After all the long, weary hours of flogging oneself into the ground one was suddenly released, allowed to take off, to leap and soar and be ecstatic. This time it was for *real*. He felt almost drunk with the glory of it. It was like knocking up the runs at cricket. *Wham!* the boundary. *Wham!* through the covers. And everyone cheering, everyone applauding –

"I told you," whispered Anita, "that you'd bring the house down!"

His exhilaration sustained him throughout the interval – it sustained him even as he struggled into the hated tights and pulled on the too-short tunic. It didn't really bother him any more, that the tights

147

were white and the tunic didn't cover anything. No one was going to laugh at him. He'd already shown them what he could do. Even his Dad was going to have to admit that there was a bit more to it than he'd originally thought.

The curtain went up again on the second half. The act opened with a thing that was described in the programme as a scena (pronounced by Miss Tucker as "shayna"), followed by a Peasant Dance, with Garstin wearing his nylon thread (it had brought him out in a rash under his arms, a fact which appeared to give him no small amount of satisfaction if the number of times he had told people about it was anything to go by), followed by a solo from a girl who everyone said was "awfully *good* – but not a patch on Anita", followed at last by the Dewdrop routine. Jamie and Anita came on right at the very end. It gave him plenty of time to get nervous again, if he was going to, but although he felt odd twinges in his fingertips and a prickling sensation in the small of his back, it was from anticipation rather than from fear. He knew now that he could do it: he just wanted to be out there, getting on with it.

The Dewdrops cantered to their accustomed halt, broke ranks and re-formed, making a framework for him and Anita. He led her on, as Miss Tucker had taught him, walking as she had taught him to walk – "Walk tall. Be conscious of yourself." From the back of the hall came the sound of not very subdued laughter. Jamie froze. He felt Anita waver slightly, and then pick up. A high-pitched voice came shrilling at him from out of the auditorium: "Hey, Jamie! What about your hands?"

It was the Baboon. The Baboon and Roy Canary. They were out there, in the darkness. They had come on purpose to jeer at him.

"Hey, Jamie . . . what about your hands?"

In his ear, he heard Anita's urgent whisper: "Ignore them! Just carry on!" He danced mechanically, his legs coming to his rescue as they had before. The thoughts went seething through his brain. The Baboon and Roy Canary! How long had they been out there? They couldn't have been there in the first half, or they'd have started on their catcalls straight away. They must have slipped in during the interval. But how had they found out? Kim had been sworn to strictest secrecy, and none of the other girls went to Tenterden; he had made very sure of that. Maybe one of them had a brother, or a sister. A brother who knew someone – a sister who was going out with someone –

"Lovely pair o' calves you got there, darlin'!"

Loud shushes, now, were coming from the audience. It would take more than shushes, thought Jamie, to shut that pair up. He felt a kind of fury seize hold of him – not so much on his own behalf, as on Anita's. This was her big moment; the moment she'd been waiting for, working for. And now these loud-mouthed apes were doing their best to ruin it for her. He had an almost overpowering urge to stop dancing, to advance upon the footlights and yell at them to "Sod off, the pair of you!"

"Keep going!" hissed Anita. "Keep going!"

It wouldn't help her if he were to yell "sod off". It might bolster his own ego, if only temporarily; but it wouldn't help Anita. Reluctantly, he thrust the impulse to one side.

"Oh! Wot a tantalizin' twirl! Proper little Nooryeff, innee? A right dark – "

The voice of the Baboon broke off in mid-sentence. There were slight sounds as of a scuffle, a door banged shut at the back of the hall; peace was restored. The remainder of the show passed without incident. If Jamie couldn't quite recapture the joyousness of the first half, he had the satisfaction of knowing that at any rate he hadn't let Anita down. The applause at the end was tumultuous; he had to lead her out four times. Her eyes were shining, her face was flushed. She was really in her element, he thought. He was glad, for her sake, that things had turned out OK.

It was a bit of a let-down, afterwards, changing back into humdrum jeans and sweater in his poky dressing room, with Garstin still rabbiting on about his rash.

"Look at it — look at it!" He held up an arm so that Jamie could peer into his armpit. "It'll take days for that lot to clear up. Say, who were those yobs I heard yelling? Some of your mob?"

"Just some casual acquaintances," said Jamie.

"Strange people you know."

"Yeah . . . it's the strange school I'm forced to go to."

He was playing it cool, in front of Garstin, but deep inside him was a black pit full of yellow-bellied slime. News travelled fast in Tenterden Road. Come Monday morning there wouldn't be a boy in the whole of Class 5 who hadn't got the message: proper little Nooryeff . . . He could imagine the sort of greeting he'd be given. He could imagine the jeers, the ribaldry, the jokes chalked up on the blackboard. As for Doug — he just didn't want to think about Doug. "Any more lip on Monday and we let 'em have it. Right?" Jamie was still prepared to let them have it; he just had this horrid feeling that he might have to do it by himself. He hoped very much that he would be proved wrong, but he certainly wouldn't be prepared to place any bets on it.

There was a tap at the door and a head poked round. It was Anita.

"Can I come in?" she said. She was already half-way through the door before she'd finished saying it. Garstin, who had got down to his underpants in his eagerness to divest himself of the nylon thread, snatched prudishly at a towel, but he needn't have bothered: Anita scarcely spared him a glance. It wasn't Garstin she had come to see.

"*Jamie!*" She hurled herself at him, flinging both arms about his neck. It took him by surprise. He was, fortunately, standing fair and square upon his feet, or the impact would surely have sent him flying. Even as it was, he staggered slightly. "Jamie, you were fantastic!" She spoke breathlessly: her eyes were still shining, her cheeks still flushed. "You ignored them – you carried on – I just couldn't believe it!"

Neither could he: he just couldn't believe it. This was really happening? It took him a second or so to recover.

"I only did what you told me to."

"Yes, but how many other people would have done? How many people would have had the *courage*? You kept everything going – you didn't even falter!"

He wondered if she knew how close he had come to holding up the action whilst he took time off to hurl invective.

"Truly," said Anita, "you were fan*TAS*tic!"

"Oh, I dunno." He shrugged a shoulder, not quite comfortable under the weight of all this unaccustomed praise. "I didn't really do anything so very great."

"*I* think you did," said Anita. "I think what you did was the bravest" – under Garstin's slightly pop-

151

eyed gaze, she went on tiptoe to press a kiss against his cheek – "the bravest thing that anyone could ever do."

She was wrong about that: the bravest thing that anyone could ever do was yet to come. It would come on Monday morning, when he had to go into school and face Doug. Still, he would cross that bridge when he came to it. This was his moment of triumph: he might as well make the most of it.

"Tell me," he said. He closed his arms about her waist. "You going home in the car, with Daddy?"

"Yes. D'you want a lift?"

"Not really . . . I was wondering if you'd fancy a bit of a walk across the Common, instead?"

Anita tilted her head back, considering the idea.

"It'll be dark," she said.

"Yeah, I know," said Jamie. "But I am very brave . . . you just said so. Of course, if you don't trust me – "

"Oh, Jamie," she said, "of *course* I do!" She suddenly broke away from him, pulling open the door with such vigour that Garstin was very nearly flattened into the wall. "Just give me ten minutes," she said. "I'll be with you."

The door banged shut behind her. Garstin emerged, grumbling.

"I never thought *she* was the type," he said.

Jamie looked at him, dangerously.

"What type?"

"Type for going potty over people," said Garstin.

"She isn't," said Jamie.

He grinned at himself, as he sat down before the mirror: he guessed you had to be pretty wonderful, for a girl like Anita to go potty over you . . .

152

ALSO IN

HEINEMANN
NEW WINDMILLS

General Editors: Anne and Ian Serraillier

Chinua Achebe Things Fall Apart
Douglas Adams The Hitchhiker's Guide to the Galaxy
Vivien Alcock The Cuckoo Sister; The Monster Garden; The Trial of Anna Cotman
Michael Anthony Green Days by the River
Bernard Ashley High Pavement Blues; Running Scared
J G Ballard Empire of the Sun
Stan Barstow Joby
Nina Bawden The Witch's Daughter; A Handful of Thieves; Carrie's War; The Robbers; Devil by the Sea; Kept in the Dark; The Finding; Keeping Henry
Judy Blume It's Not the End of the World; Tiger Eyes
E R Braithwaite To Sir, With Love
John Branfield The Day I Shot My Dad
F Hodgson Burnett The Secret Garden
Ray Bradbury The Golden Apples of the Sun; The Illustrated Man
Betsy Byars The Midnight Fox
Victor Canning The Runaways; Flight of the Grey Goose
John Christopher The Guardians; Empty World
Gary Crew The Inner Circle
Jane Leslie Conly Racso and the Rats of NIMH
Roald Dahl Danny, The Champion of the World; The Wonderful Story of Henry Sugar; George's Marvellous Medicine; The BFG; The Witches; Boy; Going Solo; Charlie and the Chocolate Factory; Matilda
Andrew Davies Conrad's War
Anita Desai The Village by the Sea
Peter Dickinson The Gift; Annerton Pit; Healer
Berlie Doherty Granny was a Buffer Girl
Gerald Durrell My Family and Other Animals
J M Falkner Moonfleet
Anne Fine The Granny Project
F Scott Fitzgerald The Great Gatsby
Anne Frank The Diary of Anne Frank

Leon Garfield Six Apprentices
Graham Greene The Third Man and The Fallen Idol; Brighton Rock
Marilyn Halvorson Cowboys Don't Cry
Thomas Hardy The Withered Arm and Other Wessex Tales
Rosemary Harris Zed
Rex Harley Troublemaker
L P Hartley The Go-Between
Esther Hautzig The Endless Steppe
Ernest Hemingway The Old Man and the Sea; A Farewell to Arms
Nat Hentoff Does this School have Capital Punishment?
Nigel Hinton Getting Free; Buddy; Buddy's Song
Minfong Ho Rice Without Rain
Anne Holm I Am David
Janni Howker Badger on the Barge; Isaac Campion
Kristin Hunter Soul Brothers and Sister Lou
Barbara Ireson (Editor) In a Class of Their Own
Jennifer Johnston Shadows on Our Skin
Toeckey Jones Go Well, Stay Well
James Joyce A Portrait of the Artist as a Young Man
Geraldine Kaye Comfort Herself; A Breath of Fresh Air
Clive King Me and My Million
Dick King-Smith The Sheep-Pig
Daniel Keyes Flowers for Algernon
Elizabeth Laird Red Sky in the Morning
D H Lawrence The Fox and The Virgin and the Gypsy; Selected Tales
Harper Lee To Kill a Mockingbird
Laurie Lee As I Walked Out One Midsummer Morning
Julius Lester Basketball Game
Ursula Le Guin A Wizard of Earthsea
C Day Lewis The Otterbury Incident
David Line Run for Your Life; Screaming High
Joan Lingard Across the Barricades; Into Exile; The Clearance; The File on Fraulein Berg
Penelope Lively The Ghost of Thomas Kempe
Jack London The Call of the Wild; White Fang
Lois Lowry The Road Ahead; The Woods at the End of Autumn Street

How many have you read?